Her eyes continued to widen until the rest of her face was a dwindling blur. Then I began to grow heavy, to sink down beneath the waves of reality foot by foot. I couldn't see her at all.

Then I did see her—but not as Bobby Jackson. I seemed to be on the opposite side of the kitchen, a foot from the door. My breath caught in my throat and I crouched lower and—Crouched! Suddenly I understood. The kitchen door had been left open and a cat had crept in and the cat was me! I had become, if only partly and in a nightmarishly split-up way, Mrs. Parker's cat. I was close to the floor and creeping toward her like an animal. My movements were slow, ungainly, and there was a scraping sound as I advanced. But she wasn't even looking in my direction. All of her attention was centered on the boy by the table and that boy was no longer me!

LEST EARTH BE CONQUERED

Frank Belknap Long

WILDSIDE PRESS

LEST EARTH BE CONQUERED

A BELMONT BOOK—December 1966

Published by
Belmont Productions, Inc.
1116 First Avenue, New York, N. Y. 10021

1 BOBBY JACKSON

IT WAS a frightening discovery. The man and woman living in the Jonathan Oakham mansion weren't human. Don't ask me what made me so sure. There are some things you can't explain, can't analyze. Like almost everybody else, I live at times in a private world of my own, and I never fail to become alarmed when something decidedly *wrong* shakes that world to its foundations.

All right, I'm only fourteen years old. But I'm a very smart boy. They say I have an I.Q. of about 150, and while a genius level I.Q. can be twenty points higher than that . . .150 suits me fine. A 150-boy can conceal most of what he knows, but the 170-boys are babes in the woods. The genius-level drive in them is *too* strong. They stick out their necks too far at too early an age and—well, you know the old saying. The goblins will get you if you don't watch out. For "goblins" substitute "average citizens."

But to get back to the Oakham mansion couple. They'd set up housekeeping in that ivy-hung old mauseleum of a place without any particular fanfare—no fuss or bother to set neighborly tongues to wagging.

They started off by picking just the right names for themselves—Mr. and Mrs. Thomas Martin. As every bird watcher knows, the martin is a gray and inconspicuous swallow, with a substantial, no-nonsense air about it. I could practically hear the neighbors saying: "With a name like that he must be in real estate or something. Even if he's loaded it's a safe bet he doesn't splurge. Probably has a son or daughter away at college somewhere. A man who wants the good things of life for his children. No big, expensive car even if he could afford it. No Jaguar-type little car either, no swanky night club or roadhouse hangovers. You can always tell."

At first glance you'd have said that Martin was in his late forties. But somehow the term "middle-aged" didn't quite fit him, and that was what first made me suspicious. Helen Martin in particular. When you looked steadily at her face in bright sunlight it seemed neither young nor old. It had a kind of ageless look.

It wasn't conspicuous. It didn't leap right out at you. But it was there, unmistakably. It was the sort of thing a boy with an I.Q. of 170 might have missed entirely. He'd have tried to be too scientific, too analytical.

The rest of the picture I'll try to fill in quickly. Just from what I've said you should have the canvas set up, the broad outlines sketched out. Your start should have this general look about it: New neighbors in the old Oakham place at last, a furniture van unloading, a smile and a pat on the head for the six-year-olds who watch everything. Then, in two or three more swift strokes of the drawing pencil—a new account at the Second National, and an immediate visit to the chain grocery, with Mr. Martin saying: "Oh. yes, you must be Mrs. Parker, who's to be our neighbor. The renting agent told us . . ." Smiles and nods all around. "Well now, isn't that fine? Mrs. Martin thought she'd better stock up on a few groceries. Butter, milk and eggs anyway. Just for tonight, you know. Tomorrow we'll have time to do some real shopping."

For about two weeks after that it's all smooth sailing. They get to know more of the neighbors, move cautiously, make themselves liked in a quiet sort of way. They are careful to see that there are no rough edges, nothing to cause a raising of eyebrows.

Thomas Martin going to work every morning with a briefcase under his arm, Mrs. Martin fussing about in the kitchen or out in the backyard hanging up wash. Smiles for the children, the tradespeople.

Can a man work somewhere in a medium-sized town and keep his occupation a secret from the neighbors? You'd be surprised. For a month or two it can be done. "Where does Mr. Martin work?" "Somewhere on Cherry Street, I believe. He doesn't talk much about his job." "Well, no—but not all of us do. He appears to be the kind of man who doesn't like to mix business with his home life. What's so unusual about that?"

That's the picture, in broad outlines. That's the picture until—I enter it.

If you like, you can visualize me as just hovering around the frame at first. I became suspicious the day they moved in, but the "wrongness" was just a faint whisper to me until I began to notice little peculiarities of behavior cropping up here and there.

Mrs. Martin staring at a basket of tomatoes in the chain grocery for instance, as if she had never seen tomatoes before. Picking them up and feeling them and misjudging their weight. Her eyes widening in astonishment as she dropped one and heard it *scrunch*.

And one incident that wasn't so minor. Thomas Martin walking down the street at nine o'clock in the morning and leaping to one side with a terrified look at a car several feet from the curb. Completely safe on the sidewalk and yet behaving as if there were a wild-eyed maniac at the wheel who wanted him dead. All the blood draining out of his face, his briefcase clutched to his chest.

7

Then there was the frightened tomcat. He belonged to Mrs. Parker and she called him "Sugar." No one knew why, because he had a vicious disposition. He would stand and fight even those big, wolflike dogs you see sometimes. If you owned a wolf and became attached to the beast you'd probably try to pass it off as a dog too, and every so often I see a dog that makes me wonder.

Sugar was wholly a cat, but there was something tigerish about him. Nothing sweet about Sugar—a spitting, clawing fury! But you should have seen him on the fence backing away from Mrs. Martin, his eyes wild with fright, his fur standing up all over him. His eyes stayed glassy and distended even when Mrs. Parker called to him from her side of the fence and succeeded in getting him down.

His refusal to come within hissing distance of Mrs. Martin was so uncharacteristic of him that Mrs. Parker felt called upon to apologize to her new neighbor for her pet's strange behavior.

"I don't know what's got into Sugar this morning. He's usually so friendly." (Friendly like a scorpion on a hot tin roof!)

There were other things, but it's time you visualized me as leaving the frame and moving straight into the picture —a rather goodlooking boy with freckles, clear blue eyes, and an extremely engaging manner. I'm not being conceited—just stating a fact. There's nothing more immature and conceited, actually, than false modesty.

I wanted Helen Martin to notice me and invite me inside the house. So I decided to become a gate-swinger.

Wait now—I know what you're thinking. Youre telling yourself that swinging on a gate is little boy stuff with a vengeance, something most kids outgrow before they're half through grammar school. Ordinarily you'd be right. But there are gate swingers and gate swingers and I've known grown men to do it.

You see, the Oakham mansion gate was big and rusty

and free-swinging—a real antique. Even a high school senior, idling along with nothing else to do, would have been tempted to swing on *that* gate. Just to test it out, just in the spirit of a lark.

It was really a gate for a man of muscle and girth, and I could picture Falstaff perched securely upon it, swinging himself back and forth with a mighty shout. Falstaff was a huge, good-natured fellow and I have much the same good-natured look, when I'm really relaxed and enjoying myself. I was quite sure that I'd look like innocence itself if I carried it off in a completely natural way.

I just had to be careful to pick the right time—when Helen Martin was out in the yard and Mrs. Parker was busy in her own kitchen, or upstairs bleaching her stringy hair or making a confident of her fiendish cat. I couldn't help thinking it was a lucky thing she'd married a man wealthy enough to support her *after* he'd left her a widow.

The right time fell on a hot August afternoon. There wasn't a breath of air stirring, and straight across the lawn from where I'd started swinging Mrs. Martin was standing in the shadow of a lilac bush, shading her eyes with both hands and looking right at me.

Ordinarily people don't shade their eyes with both hands. It blocks out the glare completely, but it's likely to attract attention if you don't want people to single you out as peculiar. Try it sometime. One thumb on each cheekbone, the fingers meeting in the middle of the forehead.

It's the best way of shading the eyes. But Helen Martin was trying to do all of the expected things and once again I'd caught her in a bad slip.

She spent only a minute or two staring at me before she started toward me across the lawn. I stopped swinging and waited for her to come within speaking distance. In a way, it was an exciting moment for me. My heart did a flip-flop and although it didn't make much sense I gave

9

the gatepost a pat, and smiled at her in a sheepish sort of way.

I knew almost exactly what she was going to say.

She said it. "You're Bobby Jackson, aren't you? The banker's son?"

Another slip. She should have said: "You're the Jackson boy, aren't you? I saw you at the bank yesterday, talking to your father." Or something of the sort. That "banker's son" with a question mark after it didn't have quite the right ring. I'm being subtle perhaps, but—well, it was like asking: "You're the baker's son, aren't you?" The baker, the cobbler, the candlestick maker. Everyone in the town has a trade, like in the Middle Ages. The medieval guild sort of thing.

It was the kind of question a visitor from Mars or Venus with no knowledge of what life in twentieth century America was like would have thought logical, because most complex societies pass through a medieval guild stage.

But of course I didn't let on that I'd caught her in a slip. I let the sheepish grin widen a little and I said: "Yeah, Mrs. Martin. I'm Bobby Jackson. I—I didn't mean to swing on the gate so hard."

She smiled then. The smile startled me, because it was so friendly, warm and ingratiating. She hadn't slipped up there. It was a completely human smile and for a moment or two her face no longer seemed strange.

"I might have known," she said. "You're the kind of boy who just couldn't resist a gate like that. It's written all over you."

"I don't usually do it," I said. "But I was wondering if it would creak if I swung myself back and forth on it, the way old gates are supposed to do. This sure is an old gate. Rusty and kind of picturesque."

It was just the right reply—I hoped. "Picturesque" is a word that fourteen-year-old boys seldom use, but I

10

wanted her to think me a rather precocious youngster. Not too much so, but alert and discerning. Just different enough to arouse her interest, and make her want to become better acquainted with me.

"I understand perfectly," she said. "You don't have to apologize. To tell you the truth, that gate fascinated me the first time I looked at the house. I'm quite sure my husband would·have swung on it, if he hadn't been such a silly old fool about his dignity. Bobby, would you like to come inside and have a cool drink of lemonade? It's an awfully hot day."

I framed my reply with care. Fourteen-year-old-boy talk now, don't overdo it, keep it a bit slangy. "Gee, that would be swell, Mrs. Martin," I said. "Lemonade would hit the spot. If it won't put you to any bother—"

"No bother, Bobby. I've got a big pitcher all made. My husband prefers claret wine diluted with water, ice and plenty of sugar. But lemonade's much nicer, really."

She turned then and I followed her across the yard and into the house. Inside it was spacious, and cool. The living room especially. If the furnishings had been selected by an interior decorator they couldn't have been in better taste.

I followed her into the kitchen and there was the lemonade—in a big pitcher with a double spout.

"Sit down, Bobby," she said. "Make yourself comfortable."

I sat down at the kitchen table and she filled two glasses right to the brim. It was another slip. You don't pour that way unless you are a little jittery and there was nothing wrong with the way she held the pitcher. The glass would spill a little when I lifted it, but apparently she hadn't given that a thought.

A crazy thought flashed through my mind. What will she say now? *Here's to you, Bobby? Mud in your eye?*

Her voice dispelled the ridiculous turn my thoughts

were taking. When you're under a strain you can become light-headed for an instant and start thinking the way you do when you're repeating nonsense rhymes. Out of Lewis Carroll, say. But the moment she said: "There's nothing like an iced drink on a hot day to cool you off, is there, Bobby?" I was back in the groove again, alert and on my toes and watching her every second.

I nodded, and she filled my glass again, all the way to the brim. Right at this point I may as well confess to something that may startle you a little, but there's no reason why it should. Every psycho-analyst worth his twenty dollars an hour knows that at thirteen or four-teen every normal boy begins to become aware of sex in a completely adult way. A fourteen-year-old boy doesn't have to have an I.Q. of 150 to be stirred by the sight of a beautiful woman moving about with seductive grace very close to him.

It is an age of sex awareness, of sex awakening. The long childhood period of latency is over, and you begin to be aware of what a beautiful thing sex can be.

A woman of thirty or thirty-five may seem almost old to a boy my age, but the stirring is there notwithstanding. And when Helen Martin moved close to me I experienced it just as intensely as if I'd been twenty-five. I had the feeling that she wasn't being consciously seductive, hadn't the remotest idea of what was passing through my mind. And that, in a way, was another slip, because she should have at least pretended to understand.

The stirring was there, but I forced myself to keep it at arm's length because if what I suspected was true, and she wasn't human it would have been dangerous for me to let sex get mixed up with any part of the investigation I was determined to make.

I kept watching her face, studying her expression, be-cause I knew how important it was to find out just how much she was concealing. If my gate-swinging perform-

12

ance had failed to deceive her inviting me inside the house would have been a wise move on her part. The only way she could get me to talk freely was to convince me of her complete sincerity. By questioning me in a friendly way she had a fair chance—or so she must have thought—of persuading me to lower my guard.

I kept watching her face and that was where I made my big mistake. *For she was watching me.*

She kept her eyes trained on me even when she picked up the pitcher and poured herself another glass of lemonade. I didn't even realize how hypnotically compelling her stare was until I tried to look away and found that I couldn't.

Maybe if I'd tried hard enough I could have broken the spell before it was too late. But she was smiling and nodding at me over the raised glass, and it took a few seconds for the fear that was creeping in my mind to flash a danger signal.

When the flash came her eyes had begun to widen, opening up like great, dark-petaled flowers and a constriction had tightened about my legs, preventing me from moving. My arms too felt numb, weighted.

Her eyes continued to widen until the rest of her face was a dwindling blur. For a moment they seemd to fill the room, growing larger and larger until I felt swallowed up in their merciless scrutiny.

For a terrifying instant I struggled to keep the eyes from breaking down all of my resistance and demolishing the only thing to which I could still cling—awareness of my own identity. I fought against becoming completely lost in that immensity of iris glimmer, against ceasing to be Robert Jackson, the son of a bank president, a boy with a will and a mind of his own who would fight to stay what he was until some horror unimaginable forced him to give up the struggle.

It was a losing battle, for all at once the eyes were

13

gone and I was enveloped in a vast and swaying blueness. I was no longer Robert Jackson. I was a frail raft adrift on a boundless ocean. The tides were pulling me back and forth, and the waves were breaking and washing over me and the terrible weight of them pressed in upon me and I felt myself to be smothering.

Then I began to grow heavy, to sink down beneath the waves foot by slow foot. Immense shadowy creatures drifted past me, hooded monsters of the deep with iridescent tentacles that came perilously close and then darted away with a long drawn swishing sound. There were other sounds. A mournful tolling, as if a distant bell were sounding a dirge and a shrill, but far-away screaming. Deeper I sank and deeper . . .

"Bobby, Bobby, wake up!" She was shaking me by the shoulders but I couldn't see her at all. I could only hear her voice pleading with me, urging me to return to the surface of that deep and turbulent sea. She was urging me to be myself again—Bobby Jackson.

I could feel her hands tugging at my shoulders as I swayed above the table, the lemonade glass still in my hand.

Then I *did* see her—but not as Bobby Jackson. I seemed to be on the opposite side of the kitchen, a foot from the door and I could see her very plainly as she kept pleading with the boy by the table to become me again.

I was close to the floor and creeping toward her like an animal. My movements were slow, ungainly, and there was a scraping sound as I advanced. But she wasn't even looking in my direction. All of her attention was centered on the boy by the table and that boy was no longer me!

How could he have been Bobby Jackson when I was staring at him from thirty feet away? He looked exactly like me. There could be no doubt of that. But it was as if I'd shaken off the identity linkage that had made me think and feel and act like Bobby Jackson and no one

14

else, and taken on a completely new identity. Even though I could remember being Bobby Jackson a moment or two before, strange, new emotions were stirring in me that filled me with horror.

Suddenly a draft from the slightly open door started to shiver along my spine and I experienced a sensation that was just as new and terrifying. My breath caught in my throat and I crouched lower and—

Crouched! The fear that making me tremble came out into the open, and faced me with green eyes ablaze, unblinkingly in a nightmare kind of half-light that was worse than total darkness. The kitchen door had been left open and a cat had crept in and the cat was me. I had become, if only partly and in a nightmarishly split-up way, Mrs. Parker's cat. That fiendish animal, treacherous beyond belief, had somehow managed to get inside Bobby Jackson's mind and undermine his identity and what I was now experiencing was a cat's awareness of itself. How could I doubt it?

I don't know just what it was that saved me. It may have been a weakening of the spell which Helen Martin had used to make me relinquish my grip on reality, for she was now making even more frantic efforts to make me become the boy by the table again. It was as if she had gone too far and realized it and was appalled by what she had done.

Or I may have been saved by a part of my mind that would not let itself be undermined, a sanity-clinging part that kept screaming at me, with a desperate urgency, that it was manifestly impossible for a human being to become one of the lower animals.

I think it was probably that, and not Helen Martin's terrified pleading, that brought me back into my own body at last.

I stirred and opened my eyes and there was Helen Martin again, looking relieved and on the verge of tears,

15

looking so nearly human that for a moment I found myself thinking of her as a nurse—a gentle, understanding nurse in a stiffly starched white uniform. Laying soothing hands on my brow, and thrusting a thermometer under my tongue and whispering: "Just rest now, Bobby. Nothing to worry about. You're going to be all right."

Then, all at once, everything became completely real and the opposite of nightmare-strange, or even dream-strange in a soothing way. Helen Martin said quietly, in a sympathetic but completely matter-of-fact voice: "It must have been the sun, Bobby. Heat exhaustion. You were swinging pretty hard on that gate, weren't you?"

"Yeah, I—I guess I was," I lied. "It was a crazy thing to do, because I've been out in the sun most of the day. I was playing basket-ball this morning, for almost two hours."

"That explains it then."

I nodded. "For a minute there everything went black."

She patted me on the shoulder and I was afraid she'd say: "You'd better go into the living room and lie down, Bobby. You mustn't think of leaving until you feel better."

I didn't want to stay in that house for another ten seconds. I didn't even want her to plead with me to stay, for there was the gravest kind of danger in just listening to her voice. I was sure of that now.

I'd never been so frightened. I'm not ashamed to admit it. I was scared the way savages are supposed to be in the presence of the unknown, the whispering forests, the ancestral dead with their rice-white faces and shambling gait.

Only—it was worse than that. Something stranger, vaster and infinitely less human—as if a destroying wind from far outer space had come into the room and was blowing cold upon me.

Her hand tightened on my shoulder and she said with

16

unmistakable concern in her voice. "Bobby, what is it? Why are you staring at me like that?"

She was pretending, of course, putting on an act and I'd come dangerously close to giving myself away. Maybe I had and it was already too late.

But I refused to let myself think that. I got up and walked toward the kitchen door, glancing back just once with a "I don't feel too good" look to make my departure seem less abrupt and perfectly natural under the circumstances.

Who'd expect a reply from a kid just recovering from a heat exhaustion blackout and wanting to get home fast? No substitute for a boy's own family at a time like that. I hoped she'd realize how I was supposed to be feeling and let me go without forcing me to do any more lying.

She did. I was out of the house and down the lane and running for my life before I heard the kitchen door slam with a bang, as if suddenly, and at the last moment, she'd tumbled to the truth and was angry at herself for letting me get away alive.

2 BOBBY JACKSON

IN A TOWN as big as Lakeview things happen in a scattered sort of way. There's no gossip grapevine that you can follow from neighbor to neighbor in a straight line. You can start almost anywhere but you have to get around fast if you're intent on gathering all the evidence

17

together in one basket before memory lapses cheat you of important items and make you feel you haven't done as much as you could.

First I did some inquiring at the post office, three or four stores, the library and the Lakeview Athletic Club. Everywhere, in fact, where the "banker's son" could count on being accorded a fair measure of adult respect. Forget the 150-I.Q. part. That was something of a handicap, but the "banker's son" more than counter-balanced it.

At times I'd even overhear comments like: "He's a swell kid. Just listens quietly to what you have to say and has a good word for almost everybody. He's bright, all right. But he never tries to take folks apart the way some kid prodigies seem to feel they're entitled to do. Yeah, that's right. They tell me he's popular at school. A great little athlete. Not one of those know-in-all youngsters with his nose always buried in a book."

I had my reservations about that kind of compliment, but I was careful not to let it show.

My inquiries brought results. But just to keep the record straight I didn't know myself at this stage precisely what kind of information I was searching for. I was still grop-ing in the dark to some extent, playing it by ear.

Don't smile. That's the best way to play it when you know, deep down, that you've latched on to something important.

I drew a complete blank in about half of the places where I played the part of a very alert youngster, eager to know more about how new residents like the Martins got on with people. I made sure it would just seem like boyish curiosity on my part, and there's no boy in the world who doesn't display that kind of curiosity at times. It doesn't make much sense when you analyze it. But it's accepted as a matter of course, simply because there's a boy buried deep in every man, and idle prying is a universal human pastime.

In about half of the places I made no progress at all and in another forty percent what I found out was run-of-the-mill information, hardly worth recording. But then I struck pay dirt. First there was talkative old Mr. Donigan at the Acme Hardware Store. Sure, Mr. Martin had dropped in, twice. Purchases? Nothing important—a tube of mend-it-yourself liquid cement and a medium-sized hammer. Did he talk to anyone besides Mr. Donigan himself? You bet he did. Will Sanders, in particular. Sanders had been leaning over a counter, staring longingly at a red-enameled pocket knife—the kind with more blades than you can count—when Martin had come into the store, edged up alongside of him and started admiring the knife too.

Now Will Sanders was a character. For one thing, he was a whittler, going right back to the cracker-barrel, general store days of a half century ago. You'll run into a few of them still, in every small town, particularly in the South. But in a medium-sized industrial town today they are practically dinosaur-extinct.

He just didn't belong to mid-twentieth century, TV-conscious America. In a half dozen ways he was a throwback, a loveable old freak. He lived all alone in a hermit-like shack at the edge of town, and raised leghorns for a living. Believe it or not, his grandfather had known Custer and had just missed being at Little Big Horn.

Martin and Sanders had talked for ten or fifteen minutes and had then left the store together, still talking like old buddies at a veteran's rally.

Anything more? No—but it went down in my little black book as important. In five of the other places I discovered this about Martin. He liked to talk to people —all kinds of people. But every native he talked to was a distinct type and unusual enough to stand out. I'll run

19

them off briefly. Fred Halstrom, who was a garage mechanic with a vengeance, the kind that bends over the uplifted hoods of cars with a look of rapture on his face, as if running in his veins was a big, bursting flood of high-octane from every car he'd ever serviced. It was the engines that got him—grease, grease, grease, and the green coppery sheen of heated tubing, and the wonderful *smell* of a real fine engine that he could tinker over until the stars fell out of the sky.

There was Samuel Thompson, athletic instructor at Lakeview High—all-around, all-American idol of the sweater-wearing, trunk-wearing bunch of Varsity-League hopefuls, who never doubt they'll make the grade at Princeton or Yale. He could pole-vault, swim, chalk up a track record and crash a goal line better than anyone I knew.

Next on the list was Clifford Andrews. Clifford was a bookworm, the kind that really makes a profession out of just boring into knowledge—not so much for enlightenment as for excitement. Dry-as-dust excitement, if you will, but even barnacles and shipworms probably have their high moments.

Then there was Theodore Murch, who works at my dad's bank. He was the medium-sized town's version of the man in the gray flannel suit. No—cross out that geographical limitation. He would have stood out as an under thirty, up-and-coming brokerage firm executive if he'd stepped into the subway at the Wall Street station in New York City.

The other two—Jake Seaton and Stanley Webb—were average citizens—except that they both overdid it. There's a kind of averageness that stands out and hits you right between the eyes, and makes you think of that line in Orwell's *Animal Farm*: "All oxen are equal but some are more equal than others."

I got home about five o'clock and went straight upstairs to my room. Mom called to me from the living room and when I didn't reply raised her voice an octave or two.

"Is that you, Bobby? Where were you all afternoon?"

That kind of questioning can be annoying, but Mom is a good sort, when you make allowances for certain basic limitations, and I felt ashamed of myself almost immediately.

I stopped at the top of the stairs and called back: "I met Freddy Jason in front of the library, and we had a couple of sodas."

"Sodas? All afternoon? Bobby, really—"

I went into my room, shut the door and batted a soft ball around a couple of times. Then I looked at myself in the mirror and was satisfied with what I saw. I've got a stubborn chin and I don't have to stiffen it artificially. It's always there when I take a quick glance at myself in the mirror.

I sat down on the edge of the bed and brooded. That's as good a word as any. Deep speculation is always a painful, long drawn-out process.

The picture was getting clearer and suddenly the truth flashed all around me, so bright it seemed outside my mind, an actual burst of illumination in the room.

They're studying us, I thought. They're here as observers. They're trying to find out as much as they can about the human race by studying men and women who are highly individualistic, who are unusual human types. They must shrewdly suspect that such men and women display, to a heightened degree, all of the shortcomings and all of the constructive energy and resourcefulness that has made Man's life on Earth a paradox and a mystery even to himself.

Studying them would be like—well, observing a fruit fly that has mutated a little, but is still in all respects a fruit fly. The very fact that such a fly would be unusual, a little different from the general run of fruit flies, would make it an ideal laboratory specimen. Assuming that the observer has exceptional insight and intelligence studying such a fly would be more rewarding and yield more information about fruit flies in general than a specimen at random.

Possibly I was just skirting the truth and guessing wrong about some of it. But I realized that I would have to pay the Martins another visit. Almost all of my doubts were gone now, but I had to have absolute proof. The danger was very great. It would have to be soon, or what had almost happened to me might happen to someone else. A man must face up to his responsibilities and that goes for a boy as well. Especially for a boy who has stumbled on something ghastly he can't possibly ignore, and go on living with himself. Until the Martins were exposed for what they were all of Lakeview was in danger, all of America—and I was almost afraid to think beyond that. I could not wait for a terrified Lakeview to take appropriate action. By then it might be too late. And how could the town be aroused and alerted if I could not back up what would seem the wildest, most improbable of stories with overwhelming convincing proof?

I was only sure of one thing. Helen Martin had done something to the basic structure of my mind that had made me doubt my own identity and share a cat's awareness of itself. For a terrifying instant I had almost become Mrs. Parker's cat, and had stared out of a cat's slitted eyes at a boy who was no longer me.

Anthropologists tell us that primitive man really believed he could be in several places at the same time. He had no sense of Time as we understand it, and could also think of himself as living in the past and in the present simultaneously. Not in the future perhaps, but only because his imaginative endowment wasn't sufficiently developed to enable him to think of the future in concrete terms.

But space and time imposed no restrictions at all on his mind, and he was as sure that he could be everywhere at once as we are sure that most sunsets will be red and that we'll all know grief and suffering before we die.

Moreover—and this is most important—he was firmly convinced he could be at the same time a human being and an animal. Actually he couldn't, of course, and must have been obscurely aware of it. But the belief —or superstition, if you prefer that term—was so strong in him that his fantasy life must have been quite extraordinary.

But what if it wasn't just a primitive fantasy-formation tendency—that feeling of identification with every part of the physical universe? What if it is a universal human faculty that has dulled and crusted over in modern man by the iron straightjacket of civilization.

Suppose—just suppose—that faculty is merely slumbering in most of us and can be awakened, jarred, touched off by a certain kind of mental probing? There could be no doubt at all that my mind had been jarred by Helen Martin's merciless scrutiny. In precisely what way I did not know, but jarred it had been.

It's hard to examine even small laboratory animals and subject them to a few preliminary tests without jarring them a little. White mice in experimental test runs often end up a quivering mass of nerves. Even microorganisms on a slide have been known to behave peculiarly at times, as if they could feel a wind from the unknown blowing cold upon them.

I got up and stared about the room. It was what most people would have called a regular boy's room, and I wouldn't have wanted it to look any other way. It's a great mistake to resist the emotional appeal of a number of things that are appropriate to your own chronological age and that you can't help liking when you don't feel any different from the average run of fourteen-year-old kids. And that was often.

There was a framed picture on the wall taken when I'd been twelve, showing me in athletic shorts toeing the mark in the Junior Track Team Finals, and a smaller photograph of Mom and Dad in a rowboat on the lake, which I'd snapped from shore with a beaten-up Hawkeye Brownie. A South American beetle as big as my fist mounted on cotton in a glass specimen case. Three college pennants and one baseball team pennant. On the mantel there was a big silver cup Dad had won playing golf, and on a table by the window a baseball glove and a dented catcher's mask. There was even a punching bag just to the right of the clothescloset which I took a swing at now and then.

I was just crossing to it when I remembered the Martin's again and a coldness crept around the base of my scalp. Again the urgent premonition came. I must find out more about them before it was too late.

I didn't say much all through supper while Mom put cold cuts and a bowl of cucumber and lettuce salad on the table, along with a glass of milk for me, and a Manhattan cocktail for Dad. Dad liked just one strong drink before his evening meal, so that the glow would remain with him all through dinner. It made him feel mellow and relaxed and that was all right with me. He talked about things that really interested me then—not about his tough day at the bank.

In case you're wondering, my orientation toward him wasn't Freudian in the least. I thought him a great guy. He was really the tweedy, college professor type who has big dreams and a fine, discriminating capacity for getting the most out of life. But through his deep sense of social responsibility he'd been sidetracked into the banking business—which was perhaps just as well for Mom and myself.

24

I didn't say anything until the meal was almost over and then I had to talk. Because—Dad exploded a bombshell. He'd been doing some speculating about the Martins himself and right out of the blue he said: "There's something damned peculiar about that Martin bloke—"

Dad liked to lapse into mock-British slang occasionally and ordinarily it amused me. But not now. Yet I had to admit that "bloke" seemed to fit Martin like a glove. A bloke from Brimingdon Braw Brawn. The kind of English country town that didn't exist anywhere outside of a James M. Barrie novel. A bloke from the starry night, somewhere out beyond the Great Nebula in Andromeda.

"What's peculiar about him, Dad?" I asked.

"Well, he has a very strange way of acting at times. He sort of—well, creeps up on people and starts asking them questions about their work, their interests."

"That's nonsense, Roger," Mom said. "You're forgetting how recently the Martins moved into the Oakham mansion. You were born in Lakeview. You never had to contend with the resistance of the local Brahmans. He's moved into a neighborhood where most of the homeowners are a little standoffish and suspicious of newcomers. He's probably just trying to be friendly and break down a few barriers. The best way of making friends fast is to talk to people about the things they're most interested in."

"It isn't so much the local Brahmans," Dad said. "Actually that neighborhood isn't so snooty. Not any more. A lot of old families lived there forty years ago, but most of them are in their graves now, along with the Oakhams. A few have grown wealthier, and moved to even more exclusive pastures. What makes it odd is that he's so infernally curious about almost everybody —not just his neighbors."

"Curious about you, Roger?"

Dad shook his head. "No, he only talked to me once

25

—when he came into the bank to open an account a few days ago. He was very formal and polite on that occasion. In fact, I had the impression he was trying to make himself as unobtrusive as possible. He's still trying to do that, in a way—posing as a very friendly, well-meaning new resident. But there's a strange look comes into his face at times, or so I've been told. I must have noticed it myself to some extent, or it wouldn't have stuck in my mind this way. He has very cold eyes —pale blue eyes that seem to look right through you."

"I've noticed that too, Dad," I said.

He looked at me reprovingly, as if that kind of instant boyish agreement was unworthy of me—as indeed it was. Dad knew me pretty well. He could tell when I was crudely fishing for information and failing to be ingenious about it.

I switched to another approach. "Dad?" I said.

"Yes, son?"

"Do you think he really works in an office in town? It seems funny no one has ever seen him entering or leaving an office building."

"I wouldn't know about that," Dad said. "He just gave his Oakham mansion address when he opened the account. You don't have to give—business references when you open a bank account. At least—it isn't absolutely mandatory, if you can supply enough information about yourself otherwise. The slip you fill out when you open a savings account is as simple as A B C. You just have to list the first names of your parents, your home address and attach a sample of your signature. With a checking account we do ask a few questions touching on the applicant's financial responsibility, whether or not he has an account at another bank et cetera. And if he can give us a business address and a reference or two—so much the better. But we don't insist that he give us his business address."

26

"Did he open a checking account," I asked.

Dad nodded. "Quite a large one. A large account is an indication of financial responsibility by itself and we don't take it for granted that anyone who puts a large sum of money in a bank has committed a felony. A bank is not a sheriff's office."

"Did he have an account at another bank?" I persisted.

Dad frowned and stared at me suspiciously. "Bobby, what is this? You're putting me through a quiz. Why?"

"Skip it, Dad. It's not important."

"I don't see why it should even slightly interest you. But if you must know—he had two previous bank accounts in Midland Beach. He lived in Midland Beach for three or four years before coming here. But I've certainly no intention of hopping a bus to Midland and asking questions about him there. Mr. Plummer happens to be my friend and it makes no sense to give a fellow bank president the idea you're a little on the psychotic side. The same goes for Mr. Streeter at Midland Savings and Loan."

Dad was becoming more than a little angry: I could see that and it should have given me pause. But I went right on sticking out my neck.

"Why didn't you pin him down when he opened the account," I said. "Couldn't you have asked him exactly what kind of business he was in?"

"I didn't get a chance. Murch put the account through. He only remembers filling out the form and not a goddam thing otherwise about that interview."

"Roger, *please*," Mom interposed. "Do you have to, in front of Bobby?"

"Yes, I have to. He wouldn't respect me otherwise. He knows he's asking a lot of damfool questions for no reason at all, just because I happened to mention that something about Martin aroused my curiosity. Isn't that so, son?"

27

"Sure," I said. "Dad's a human being, Mom. What the hell—"

Mom looked away quickly, because she didn't think what I'd just said was funny. I guess it wasn't. But I had to defend Dad's right to use strong language when the occasion called for it. My right as well.

I was feeling it too, sharing it with Dad. Martin's strangeness, coldness—his apartness from every other man in Lakeview. I was feeling it ten times as deeply, because of what I knew. I had swung on a gate and been carried much further than he had toward the cold, dark core of the mystery.

3 JOHN DYSON

PROBLEM KIDS! For some reason it's taken for granted today that no school is without them. But I like to think that tucked away somewhere in a green and peaceful valley, with white steeples gleaming in the distance, there is a school where learning is pursued for its own sake and the teacher is looked upon as a guide, counsellor and friend.

Maybe some day I'll take a hickory stick and go hiking off into the hills in search of it. But just for the record —I've never thought of myself as the victim of an injustice that could be remedied by turning back the clock, or making drastic changes in the educational system.

When they collect my ashes and put them in an urn some kook may take it into his head to defend me obliquely in a magazine article captioned: "How Eighth Grade Frustrations Are Lowering the Life Expectancy of Our Better Teachers," and I wouldn't want that kind of obituary to go unanswered.

Actually, I've never thought of myself as either a particularly good or a particularly bad teacher. I just like kids and try my best to understand them, and bring to the task as much pragmatic knowledge and wisdom as I've managed to pick up, in a random sort of way, across the years.

I'm largely self-educated, but some eight years ago I picked up a little knowledge in college as a long-distance runner, by majoring in educational psychology, and sprinting across the graduate school finishing line just in time to snatch the last MA they were handing out that season. Getting my breath back was another problem. I still haven't completely solved it, and anyone who has the mistaken idea that knowledge and wisdom are twin branches of the same sturdy oak should spend just one year trying to persuade fourteen-year-old kids to place a slight curb on their aggressive impulses, and think and act creatively.

I can't call Bobby Jackson a problem kid exactly, because I've never had to worry about his behavior in the classroom. But when he's given a homework assignment that would keep most kids occupied half the night—about twice a month I become a reluctant tyrant in that respect —I always have the feeling that it takes him less than an hour to breeze through the task and come up with the right answers. Not only is his homework always scrupulously neat and preceise—it has a "labored over" look.

I can't define exactly what I mean by a "labored over" look, but I can spot it every time. A kid can be a mathematical wizard or excel in English composition and if he's skimping on the time he devotes to his homework

29

it just won't have that look, no matter how letter-perfect it is in other respects.

Bobby Jackson seemed to be always boasting, whenever I caught his eye: "You see! You can't pick flaws in anything I do. You think I'm deceiving you in some way and you're very unhappy about it. But if I am . . . why should it disturb you so much?"

At such times I've often been seriously tempted to ask him to come to the desk, put him at his ease in friendly man-to-man fashion, and say to him: "Let's take off the gloves, Bobby. I'm your friend and you know it. But you're keeping something back and that isn't good at all in a teacher-pupil relationship. There's nothing wrong with short-cuts, if you have the ability to deliver. But you're making a mystery of your ability to deliver. You're using it as a bone of contention between us. You're playing a game with me, and I honestly feel I deserve something better than that."

But . . . what would have been the use?

Despite the fact that Bobby Jackson is just a tousle-haired kid who looks no older than his years he can summon to his aid all of the dignity and reserve of a corporation executive with graying temples. I could picture him smiling sadly and giving me to understand, with an admonishing shake of his head, that he was wearing no gloves, and there was no way I could prove there was the slightest antagonism between us . . . at least on his part.

To accept what can't be changed is to go against the grain at times, but it is certainly the beginning of wisdom, as any wise philosopher, ill-met by moonlight, will tell you.

All of which takes me right back to Bobby's homework again. The assignment I gave the class yesterday was distinctly on the unusual side. The space program is something no teacher can ignore, even when he'd prefer to devote the few precious moments he can snatch for serious reading to Elizabethan poetry or Walden Pond, and let books of technilogical science stay on the shelf.

So I decided to see how the class would fare if I asked them to go with me to Mars, in a spacecraft large enough to accommodate the entire class. "With me" rather than "entirely alone," because whenever youngsters are presented with an English composition challenge that really makes them toe the mark the teacher is always present, hovering in the background of each young mind as a friendly counsellor or—a pursuing nemesis with a teeth-gnashing hatred of mistakes in spelling and syntax. Sometimes a battle goes on, and they can't quite make up their minds as to how tolerant and understanding I'll be when I get down to actually grading the papers. When that happens they have been known to give me the benefit of the doubt and adopt a wait-and-see attitude.

I was pretty sure I'd have to grade at least a third of the compositions C or D, and was agreeably surprised when most of them turned out to be remarkably good. Apparently just the thought of going out into space and exploring unknown worlds makes nine kids out of ten more alert and imaginative, enlarging their horizons and enabling them to shine, both as classroom orators and on paper. In fact, eight or ten of the compositions were so excellent that they strengthened my belief that when we settle down to appraising, in a serious way, what the Space Age has done to human thinking a new look at our shopworn educational theories should be the first order of business.

But excellent as some of the compositions were, Bobby's was the only one I read over three times, with mounting admiration, before stamping it with an A.

This time he had really surpassed himself—gone all out in an effort to startle me. And in a way, despite my

31

admiration, it added fuel to the way I felt about him. Whatever standard of values a teacher may set for himself, the presence of just one student in a classroom who likes to play guessing games can be a hindrance and a snare. Fourteen-year-olds imitate what they can't understand and just the look in a teacher's eyes can be a dead giveaway.

It wasn't hard to imagine how their thoughts would run. "If Bobby Jackson can cause him to drop erasers and break chalks and pop up out of his chair like a jumping jack with his crazy questions, why can't we?"

Bobby's questions were always the opposite of crazy, of course. But how could they be expected to know that when most of what he said when he got to his feet to talk went completely over their heads?

This time I had to exercise more caution than usual to remain outwardly calm. Bobby had turned in a classic description of what Mars *must* be like. By analyzing every aspect of the 1965 Mars-probe photographs and filling in the missing parts of the puzzle with a logic that—to me, at least—was irrefutable he had left the experts far behind or out on a sagging limb.

He had described exactly the kind of dead-world landscape the first astronaut to set foot on Mars would be almost certain to encounter, and the description wasn't just something he could have drawn out of a hat without knowing what he was talking about. If he'd been that astronaut himself he couldn't have done any better.

A for Bobby then and the instant I'd read and stamped his composition I could see by his expression that he knew what was passing through my mind.

"All right, youngster," I told myself. "We're going to have a showdown, the instant the class is dismissed. You're too brilliant to be real, but you *are* real, and the paradox has to be resolved or I'll be taking *Seconal* eight or ten times a week."

32

I waited until the big clock on the supermarket tower at Anderson's Crossing tolled three times—it never fails to get a few seconds' jump on the school dismissal bell —and as soon as the class started filing out I caught Bobby Jackson's eye again and gestured for him to remain in his seat.

We didn't exchange another glance until the classroom was so silent I could hear the boughs outside scraping against the windowpanes as the wind rose and fell. It was a gusty autumn day and I could picture the rest of the kids hop-Scotching it across the school yard with the carefree abandon of small savages on a jungle trail, given leave by their elders to climb trees, turn somersaults and chase small, furry animals through the forest gloom.

I don't know why I pictured them in that way, because they could play baseball and watch TV and do a lot of other things small savages knew absolutely nothing about.

They only seemed jungle-primitive when I compared them to Bobby Jackson, who was looking at me now as if he'd read every book in the Elm Street lending library and was wondering what I'd say if he told me he was thinking of writing a few himself just to fill out the shelves.

I pretended to busy myself with the papers on my desk for a minute or two before I looked up and beckoned to him. "Bobby, I was rather astonished just now when I looked over your composition," I said. "I didn't want to discuss it with you in front of the class. That was foolish, perhaps, but—well, it seemed unfair to single out just one student's work for praise when all of the compositions were so far above average that I still haven't quite recovered from the shock."

I felt proud of myself when I saw how quickly he got up and came toward my desk, with a look of complete understanding in his eyes. I'd unbent just enough, tossed out exactly the right kind of preliminary bait. I'd let him know the other students gave me a jolt whenever they surpassed themselves and that was something he could understand and sympathize with.

When a teacher unbends to that extent he is taking a certain risk. But with Bobby I felt that the risk was minimal. He had the wit and wisdom to respect a confidence and to realize as well that a teacher can be entirely human without impairing his dignity or upsetting the pedagogical apple cart.

"Did you like the way I ended it?" he asked, all eagerness now, and without the slightest trace of antagonism in his voice.

"I liked it very much," I said. "Toward the end you gave your imagination free rein. But there's nothing wrong with that."

He looked so pleased that I felt guilty about applying the strategy I'd worked out. But there was nothing to be gained by making him think I'd delayed his departure solely to compliment him.

"Bobby," I said, leaning a little forward and looking him straight in the eye. "I wish you'd level with me—just this once. Precisely how long did it take you to complete—I'd almost said "romp through"—this Martian probe analysis? Two hours—three?"

His response wasn't quite as reciprocal as I'd hoped it might be. The always slightly stubborn set of his chin became more pronounced and a little of the antagonism came back into his voice.

"I wasn't watching the clock," he said. "About four hours, I guess."

"But it all came right out of your head?" I persisted relentlessly. "You didn't consult a single reference work as you went along?"

"You don't always have to," he said, defiantly.

"Perhaps not, Bobby," I conceded. "A Mount Wilson astronomer with a splendid memory might be able to write about Mars as accurately as you've done without consulting a reference work and double-checking his data. But I think you'll agree that in your age group that level of brilliance is extremely rare."

"I may have made a few minor errors," he said, defensively. "I haven't got a really good memory, Mr. Dyson. I'm always forgetting things."

"I wish I could say that gets you off the hook," I told him. "Unfortunately it doesn't. You can make mistakes and be absentminded and still be a genius. And there are different kinds of memory recall. Apparently even Einstein was quite capable of forgetting his umbrella or going out into a blizzard without an overcoat."

He seemed to realize that he'd been defending himself too emotionally, for he made an abrupt attempt to sidetrack my challenge by down-grading his composition in a more general way.

"You asked us to try to imagine how we'd feel if we were on a spacecraft bound for Mars and what we'd see when we got there. I didn't try to be too scientific. I just thought it would be a good idea to bring in the Martian probe photographs. People should be even more excited about them than they are. In a way . . . the transmission of actual photographs of another planet across so great a distance is almost as great an achievement as the first moon landing will be."

I happened to agree with him about that. But I merely nodded, and was on the point of reminding him that he was evading my question when I decided to confront him with a more direct challenge.

"Bobby," I asked. "Why do you do it."

"Do what, Mr. Dyson?"

"Try to keep me guessing as to just how brilliant you really are. I think you know what I mean. If you don't . . . it would not do any good to draw you a diagram."

He stared at me for a moment in silence and I could see that I'd given him a decided jolt. It's one thing to know a deliberately adopted attitude toward a friend— or an enemy—has been interpreted correctly; quite another to be confronted with that knowledge as a verbal challenge.

I knew the gloves were on again when he said: "I'm not so brilliant, Mr. Dyson. Really I'm not."

"I'm afraid I can't agree with you," I said. "Do you know what I think?"

He started to reply, but I went on so quickly that all he could do was to continue to stare at me with a look of growing antagonism in his eyes. "I think you're afraid I'll discover just how different you are from the other students and hold it against you. So you walk a kind of tightrope in your homework, and whenever I call on you in class you answer my questions in a very few words. You talk a little more when your curiosity gets the better of you and you want to find out if my ideas are in accord with your own. But that's something you can't help doing and it worries you afterwards. I can always tell when you're reproaching yourself for having said too much."

I could see that he was still determined not to yield an inch of ground, and decided I'd have nothing to lose if I made a slight strategic retreat. "Well . . . suppose we put all that aside for the moment," I said. "It was this particular composition I wanted to discuss with you. We've agreed, at least, that the ending was brilliantly imaginative."

It was true, of course. He had really let himself go imaginatively in the last few pages. Why not encourage him to talk freely about just the last part of his composition?

I was waging a kind of psychological warfare with

36

Bobby and if a teacher wants to find out exactly what makes an exceptional pupil tick there's nothing more enlightening than a free association test.

"You certainly went a little beyond what I had in mind when I discussed the assignment," I said. "You seem to feel that Mars is a completely dead world and that life as we know it could not possibly have evolved on a planet that so closely resembles the moon. But you speculate as to the possibility that it might have been used as a base . . . for perhaps hundreds of thousands of years . . . for *flying saucer* visitors from another star system. Surely you don't really believe that. To take such a possibility seriously—"

"Not just Mars alone," Bobby said, before I could go on. "Venus as well—and possibly all of the other planets. That would eliminate at least one of the stumbling blocks that keep so many people from taking flying saucers seriously . . . the major stumbling block, in fact. They may have crossed space from another star in the remote past and not have to go and return constantly."

"Or they may have just arrived," I said.

"Yes . . . that's a possibility too," Bobby conceded. "But in any case, using the Solar System's planets as a base would give them a secure foothold."

"I said I approved of your giving your imagination a free rein, Bobby. In English composition the development of imaginative talents is of supreme importance. Later on, I planned to give the class a more strictly scientific assignment to test their technological competence in the handling of data I would have supplied—at least in part. But this time I just didn't care if they engaged in some pretty wild flights of fancy. But you seem to take the flying saucer nonsense seriously—to really believe that it isn't nonsense at all. And that disturbs me a little."

"Just why do you think it's nonsense, Mr. Dyson?"

37

he countered. "Almost every day there's a new report of a UFO sighting—"

"Do you honestly expect me to take a single one of them seriously?" I asked. "There are many ways of accounting for what the eye-witnesses claim they saw. Ever since I was your age—and younger—I've seen all kinds of mysterious lights in the sky. But I've never given them a second thought. The aurora borealis, searchlights playing across the sky, the reflections on low-lying clouds of the headlights of moving cars can dance and weave about and assume all kinds of shapes—even the disklike shape that a flying saucer is supposed to have."

"But in some of the sightings eye-witnesses have claimed the UFO's move at incredible speeds, in military flight formation," Bobby said. "And a few—not many, but a few—of the photographs have been impressive."

"How impressive, Bobby?" I asked. "You're forgetting how easy it is to fake a photograph. Double exposures have an almost miraculous way of bringing ghosts out of nowhere to look over the shoulders of living men and women. I've sometimes made group pictures and forgotten to wind the camera and found that each of the sitters had an astral double.

"What you can do with landscapes is even more startling," I added, hoping to draw him into an argument that would make the battle lines stand out more clearly. "If you use special filters and experiment a little with lights and shadows you can make almost any barren stretch of countryside look ghostly and mysterious, with strange lights in the sky. What surprises me is how unimaginatively most of the flying saucer photographs appear to have been faked. They show only scattered points of light."

"It's almost impossible to fake a photograph that can withstand painstaking technological analysis," Bobby said ... and I knew, of course, that he was right. "A simple

38

double exposure wouldn't fool the experts for an instant."

"I hope you don't actually believe in little green men, Bobby," I said.

"There's no particular reason for them to be either little or green," he said.

It was practically an admission that he took the whole thing seriously. I hadn't expected him to go as far as that, and for a moment I was at a loss for words.

"It's a mistake to be too skeptical, Mr. Dyson," he said. "When so many people—"

"Just a minute, Bobby," I said. "Not too many people. Don't deceive yourself on that score. Did you ever stop and ask yourself how the overwhelming majority of people would feel if they thought they were being watched, spied upon night and day by visitors from another world? It does no harm to speculate about it, to concede that it might be just barely possible. But to be absolutely sure of it, to accept it as something you've got to live with day in and day out—"

I looked at him accusingly, hoping he'd realize how hard it was for me to believe he could have discussed flying saucers at all without taking into consideration that aspect of the problem.

Perhaps he had, and was keeping it a secret from me— to give him more room to maneuver.

"Don't you see, Bobby," I went on. "We'd never know what a visitor from another world might decide to do about human life on Earth. From day to day there would be that terrible uncertainty, the dreadful feeling that we were completely at the mercy of an alien intelligence with inscrutable endowments—an intelligence alert to every change in our daily lives. How could humanity as a whole carry on normally under such circumstances?"

The windowpanes were rattling steadily now, and the sun had either passed behind a cloud or it was darkening up for rain. There is something dismal about a classroom when the students have filed out, and a teacher finds himself alone with his thoughts. The presence of Bobby should have lessened that dismalness a little, but somehow it didn't. Why, I wondered, had I asked him to remain when our talk would probably end with his becoming more of an enigma than ever?

I suddenly had the feeling that I would accomplish nothing, that he would score a victory and walk out of the classroom with a defiant shake of his head, perhaps even blaming me for keeping him after school in a thunderstorm when he didn't have an umbrella and would be certain to get drenched. If it did rain, that is. I hoped it wouldn't.

He was looking at me now with a slightly quizzical expression on his face, as if he was at a loss to understand why I'd stopped right in the n iddle of what I'd started out to say. I paused an instant longer, picking up Bobby's composition, dividing it in the middle and setting it down again, as if I were cutting a pack of cards—solely to make certain I wasn't allowing myself to be hurried.

"The threat of thermonuclear destruction is bad enough for most of us to have to live with," I said. "But what do you suppose would happen if every man, woman and child on Earth became absolutely convinced they were under nonhuman surveillance? Could they plan for the future with any confidence, could they delude themselves into thinking they could go on as they've been doing— creating, loving, hating and—yes, even dying with the assurance, at least, that if man is to destroy himself the decision will rest with him alone?"

"I don't think everything would stop, Mr. Dyson," Bobby said.

If the world had come to an end right at that moment Bobby's confident surmise could not have been more instantly demolished. The roll of thunder was like eight or ten mortar shells exploding, and the flash of forked light-

40

ning which precedes the cannonade by the barest instant was the brightest I'd ever seen. It didn't vanish when the thunder ceased to reverberate, but came right into the classroom.

One of the forks broke off, and darted ceilingward and ran twice around the room just under the ceiling without ceasing to be blindingly incandescent. The other turned into a fireball and went spiraling toward Bobby and hovered for a terrifying instant directly over his head.

It was then that everything seemed to stop—the wind that had been rattling the windowpanes, the steady pounding of my heart and even Bobby himself. He seemed more than merely terrorstruck. There was something unnatural about his rigidity, and the ghastly pallor that had overspread his face.

It was as if he had become a figure of stone incapable of moving or crying out. Only his eyes moved, turning upward as though dazzled by the radiance of the fireball that continued, for a full minute, to hover in the air above him. Then it was gone. It did not dart away, but dwindled to a tiny pinpoint of light, and vanished in a puff of smoke and with a slight sizzling sound, such as the flame of a candle makes when it is pinched out with a wet thumb.

Slowly Bobby came back to life. But there was a look of stark terror in his eyes that lingered on, and did not vanish as the fireball had done.

He was trembling violently and so close to collapse that if I hadn't leapt up quickly and thrown a supporting arm about his shoulder I'm sure he would have gone stumbling forward and crumpled to the floor at the foot of the desk.

His lips opened and closed but the faint whispering sound he managed to make no more resembled speech than the unheard sobs of a grievously stricken, lost child in a world of no sound. Then a convulsive shudder passed

41

over him and he spoke a few words distinctly, and there was something about the helpless small boy look that he trained on me, as if in desperate appeal, that made me nod and keep nodding in an equally desperate attempt to reassure him.

It was a hopeless attempt, for the strangeness of what he'd said had made me the opposite of assured.

"They must have known . . . they must have been watching. That wasn't a lightning bolt. . . ."

I certainly didn't think it could have been anything else. There's nothing more freakish than the display which a powerful charge of electricity can produce when the atmosphere acts as a conductor. A lightning bolt can shatter a single small metal object, zigzag in all directions and spare a vast complex of machinery. Sleet and fire and candlelight are infinitely less unpredictable, and people have been "struck" by lightning and remained unharmed amidst a blinding incandescence.

No—it wasn't taking what Bobby had said seriously that had given me such a jolt. It was something quite different. His words had startled and alarmed me, but not because of what had happened. The lightning could be dismissed as simply a rather unusual manifestation of a freak thunderstorm's total unpredictability. What could not be dismissed was Bobby's emotional reaction. He had been in very great danger for an instant, was lucky to be alive. He should have been overwhelmed with relief. Instead his terror had continued to mount and he had muttered something wild that made no sense.

Had something happened to his mind? What could he possibly have meant by "they?" It had grown very dark outside now, and I was sure that in another moment the rain would come. Why hadn't he waited for another crash of thunder before deciding that something unnatural had taken place?

His shoulders were jerking now and he was holding

42

fast to my arm as if he expected a trumpet of doom to sound at any moment. If the walls had burst into flame he couldn't have looked more terrified.

"Bobby," I pleaded. "Get a grip on yourself. You're all right now. There's nothing to fear—"

It was several minutes before the look of fright went out of his eyes. He kept staring toward the window, and although I couldn't be sure I had the feeling that he was hoping against hope that a sudden cloudburst would put an end to all uncertainty.

I was hoping the same thing, because it seemed unlikely that anything short of another thunderclap and raindrops spattering against the pane would calm him. I didn't need to be convinced, but that didn't mean I wanted the sun to come out either.

Let it rain and let the thunder peal again. It was the only way a freakish lightning bolt that had almost killed a frightened boy could be fitted neatly into the pattern of a suddenly arising summer thunderstorm. Standing by itself it seemed somehow more disturbing, even though lightning and thunder without rain was by no means an unusual occurrence.

There was no rain, and after a few minutes it began to grow lighter again outside the window. But that no longer worried me, for a great change had taken place in Bobby. He had mastered his fear and was looking at me as if he was ashamed of having allowed so small a thing as a near brush with death to scare him.

I reminded him of what he'd said, not even trying to keep concern out of my voice. "What did you mean by: *They must have known . . . They must have been watching?*" I asked.

He stared at me as if he were hearing his own words for the first time, and he didn't like the way they sounded.

"I couldn't have said anything like that, Mr. Dyson," he assured me. "You must have been mistaken. I was

43

frightened, all right, and I could see that you were. But I don't remember saying anything at all."

So he couldn't remember. Well . . . perhaps he couldn't. But it seemed unlikely and I found myself wondering whether he really wanted to remember. Or perhaps—he was afraid to remember.

"You also said that it wasn't a lightning bolt," I persisted. "What made you think it wasn't?"

"I can't remember saying that either, Mr. Dyson."

"I see. Do you believe it was a lightning bolt now?"

"Of course," he said. "What else could it have been?"

It darkened up, as if it were getting ready to rain. Lightning sometimes comes out of a clear sky, in the middle of the winter. Just one sharp crack of thunder and a very bright flash of lightning."

"I know," I said, nodding. "It's usually right overhead and loud enough to wake the dead. You think for a minute the whole house has been struck. Then you remember that it's December and you just can't believe it. Was that the way you felt just now—even though it's not December?"

I was hoping he'd forget himself and say something irrational again. But he didn't walk into the trap.

"Not exactly," he said. "I thought the lightning had struck a tree in the yard. But when it came right into the classroom I was too scared to think at all."

"All right, Bobby," I said. "I guess we'd better call it a day. You were in great danger for a moment. You were aware of that, I imagine, and hardly realized what you were saying. When you're badly frightened . . . the mind can play strange tricks."

Five minutes later I was sitting alone at the desk, wondering whether I had an emotionally disturbed as well as a brilliant Bobby Jackson to worry about. He'd left with no further attempt to make me believe that whatever I seemed to think he'd said had been completely

44

blotted from his mind . . . even though it could well have been on the wild side.

I was probably allowing it to disturb me more than it should. But if Bobby was in danger, despite his brilliance, of becoming an estranged or alienated youngster it was my obligation as a teacher to see that the tendency was nipped in the bud. Life can become so unbelievably complex at times and people can do and say such extraordinary things that it's very hard to take strange behavior patterns for granted. I get worked up about them, become emotionally involved. And when your job is exacting and you haven't nearly enough time to turn serious matters over in your mind and come to a sober conclusion about them you suffer accordingly.

4 BOBBY JACKSON

I'D MADE two unfortunate mistakes in one day, but when I balanced them against what I'd accomplished I didn't feel too badly about them.

The first mistake really went back six months but it took on a new dimension when Mr. Dyson kept me in, after school and asked me some difficult-to-answer questions. The mistake started, of course, when I adopted the wrong attitude toward Mr. Dyson at the start of the school term. Ambivalence is always dangerous and sometimes it can be disastrous. I should have either made no attempt to conceal the fact that I have a genius-level I.Q. or consistently behaved like an average, run-of-the-mill student. But even with a genius-level I.Q. that can be a very tall order, particularly when you have to deceive, day after day, a teacher as discerning as Mr. Dyson.

I don't exactly know why I felt I had to deceive him. I admired and respected him and I should have realized that he was incapable of betraying a confidence. But I guess caution has become so deeply ingrained in me that I can't help behaving foolishly at times. The worst of it is—he now thinks I've been playing a kind of guessing game with him. I even let myself become a little angry when he questioned me too closely, and that was certainly the height of folly.

My second mistake could have been even more serious. When the lightning bolt came right into the classroom I was so frightened I blurted out something that must have made him explore, however furtively, the possibility that Bobby Jackson might be harboring the germs of mental illness.

I was far from sure then—and I'm still not sure—that I wasn't in the deadliest kind of danger, and not just from a freakish bolt of lightning. The roll of thunder was heard within a radius of several blocks, and the sky had darkened up a little. But what does that prove? It certainly wasn't a full-blown summer thunderstorm. What if all the questions I've been asking around town the past week, and the five times I've shadowed Mr. Martin made them decide to—

Kill me with a lightning bolt that didn't come out of a storm cloud at all but was artificially created to seal my lips forever? I've been trying very hard not to believe that. But it keeps coming back into my mind and if Mr. Dyson thought that too—after what I'd been saying to him about flying saucers it wasn't inconceivable—he would also be in danger. I didn't think he did, however. In fact, I was quite sure of it. It was the mental illness possibility that was troubling him. I could tell by the

46

way he'd looked at me when I'd swung about on my heels and walked out of the classroom.

To plant any kind of suspicion in his mind was the last thing I would have wanted to do. So naturally I denied having blurted out a few words that must have seemed to him completely wild. Whatever he thought now wasn't too important, if I was very careful not to forget myself that way again. He'd said himself that a bad fright could play strange tricks with the mind and make people mutter incoherently for a minute or two.

Two bad mistakes—but I'd accomplished a great deal to offset them on the opposite side of the ledger. Not only had I successfully shadowed Mr. Martin five times—I'd discovered exactly where he could be found between the hours of twelve and one on Mondays, Wednesdays and Fridays.

Methodical habits, rigidly adhered to, must have seemed to him of supreme importance in establishing the kind of neighborhood image he'd set out to create, for to the best of my knowledge he hadn't once failed to arrive at the Betsy Winstock Coffee Shop and Luncheonette on the dot of twelve three times a week over a period of two months.

It was located on Wilmot Street and was the second most patronized lunchroom in town. I happened to know one of the waitresses quite well and that gave the bright side of the ledger an even more promising look. I was on my way there now and didn't anticipate any difficulty in renewing a friendship that I had allowed to lapse for the better part of a year.

I was pretty sure that Miss Enslow would welcome me with an instant smile and be her usual cordial self, and I wasn't even slightly disappointed. The moment I entered the luncheonette and sat down at the long counter which ran parallel with eight glass-topped tables set end

47

to end she said: "It's been a long time, Bobby. I've missed you."

She reached over the counter and gave my hand a squeeze.

"Careful, Miss Enslow," I said. "You'll give me ideas."

She laughed and crinkled her nose at me, never doubting for a moment that I had a schoolboy crush on her. She knew I didn't look a day over fourteen. But I've never yet met a lunch-counter waitress who couldn't make a male admirer from eight to eighty forget his chronological age if she set her mind to it.

There was certainly no harm in it, and since life in a medium-sized town can turn as dull as pewterware at times I always feel grateful when anyone as attractive as Miss Enslow adds a few years to my age, if only in fun.

Ten minutes later she was setting an apple pie down in front of me and pouring me a second cup of coffee. "You like it with cream and two lumps of sugar, don't you, Bobby?"

I nodded glumly, because this time Mr. Martin hadn't arrived on the dot—it was fifteen minutes past twelve—and I was beginning to fear that he was going to break his month-long schedule because he was aware that I was willing to expose myself to danger to see just how far he'd go. A luncheonette near the center of Lakeview, on a bright September day, wasn't a very good place to conduct another lightning bolt experiment and it was just possible he'd thought of that and preferred to bide his time.

Don't give me too much credit for reckless courage. I was there more to prove to myself that my fears were groundless and that the lightning bolt had been a freak thunderstorm phenomenon and nothing more. I was hoping he hadn't the least idea I'd been shadowing him for a week and asking a great many questions. It was terribly important for me to know whether my visit to

48

the Oakham mansion had caused him to believe that I'd gone there because I suspected his secret, and should be kept under constant surveillance. It was possible that Mrs. Martin hadn't even described me to him and that he would fail to recognize me as the hare-brained youngster who had swung on a gate and made a great deal of unnecessary trouble for his wife. If she hadn't considered me a menace there would have been no need for any further concern on her part—or on his.

"You don't seem quite yourself this morning," Miss Enslow said, as if my somber mood had communicated itself to her. "Sure, and where's the fine Irish wit that used to come bubbling right up out of you?"

She knew that I was no more Irish than she was. But if it amused her to talk that way what right had I to spoil it for her?

"I guess I'm growing older and more serious," I said. "It's funny, though. No one else seems to notice it."

She looked at me and her eyes grew thoughtful. "That's true, Bobby," she said. "You always seemed much older than your years and I'd rather talk to you than—well, anyone I know."

"That's because we both know what's going on," I said. "Very few people do."

"Go right on talking, Bobby," she said. "It sounds wonderful, coming from you. People who know what's going on aren't the kind of people I admire, particularly. But I know you didn't mean it in that way."

I wasn't quite sure just how I'd meant it. But talking kept me from thinking and worrying too much, and when she asked: "What do you and I know that no one else does, Bobby?" I decided to give the conversation another nudge forward.

"I didn't say 'no one,' Miss Enslow," I reminded her. "I said 'very few people.' We're not the only smart apples in Lakeview. But we know what the score is most of the time. It's something you have to work at, though. It isn't handed to you on a silver platter."

"I see what you mean, Bobby," she said, crinkling her nose at me again. "It takes experience. There was a time when I didn't know the first thing about men. But after talking to you—"

"I'm serious about what I just said," I told her. "Everyone has a few secrets they're dead set on keeping to themselves. If they like and trust you they'll sometimes let you get a quick glimpse of them, but not before they've tidied them up a little. To really know the score you've got to put two and two together for yourself. There's no other way."

"Now you're scaring me," she chided. "What do you know about me, Bobby? Have I given myself away very often?"

"You'd be surprised," I said.

"All right, tell me. I may as well know the truth about myself."

"You do know . . . or you wouldn't be so afraid I may have guessed a secret you've kept from everybody since you were—well, my age.

"There's nothing really bad about it," I added reassuringly. "But you think it makes you different from almost everybody else and nobody likes to be *that* different."

"I don't know what you're talking about," she said. But I could tell she was lying by the deep flush that had crept up over her cheeks.

"I think you do," I said. I stirred my coffee, because all of the sugar had settled to the bottom, and smiled at her over the cup.

"Ever since you were a little girl you've gone your own way without trying to compete with anyone," I said. "You've always been just yourself. You stand off and look at yourself and are amused, and you smile at all the silly or stupid things people do, and never hold it

50

against them. You are you, and they are they, and you know, deep down, that what is happening to you is no more or less important than what is happening to them. You know you can't change people or the world very much and you long ago made up your mind that you wouldn't even try. If others try—and sometimes succeed perhaps—that is all right with you. There's certainly nothing bad about that, and you're making a mistake to feel so guilty about it."

I knew I'd said too much when I saw that she was looking at me as if I'd just made a magician's pass which turned her head to glass and could see the whole complex network of thoughts and emotions in the depths of her mind.

I can do that sometimes—not in quite that way, of course—but I don't make a practice of going around advertising it. I'd told her nothing but the truth about herself, but she'd start wondering about me now. There wasn't a trace of malice in her nature, and I was sure she suffered agonies of remorse every time she had to swat a fly. (There were three, I noticed, buzzing around the counter now which the proprietor would expect her to swat.) But just the fact that the Betsy Winstock Coffee Shop and Luncheonette was the second most popular restaurant of its kind in town meant that I had planted seeds of suspicion in very dangerous soil. She'd be almost certain to let something damaging about me slip out unconsciously now—whenever the conversation turned to "that rather precocious youngster, Bobby Jackson. You know, the banker's son."

She didn't say anything for a moment, just continued to stare at me as if I'd set down on the counter a dozen medals I'd won playing chess, and was fumbling in my pocket for a pipe and a crumpled sheet of mathematical equations I'd promised to work out for the Atomic Energy Commission.

51

For some peculiar reason which I've never been able to fathom people don't like to be told the unvarnished truth about themselves, even when it's on the shining side of the ledger. So I wasn't surprised when she said: "Bobby, you've much too wise a head on your shoulders for a boy your age. Would you like another cup of coffee?"

A boy my age! I could have reminded her that a moment before she'd practically taken it for granted that if we were speeding around a hairspin curve in a red Jaguar I'd be quite capable of taking my hand off the steering wheel and slipping it around her waist.

But I'd startled her enough already and the damage was done. "Do you want another cup of coffee?" really meant: "Bobby, please get lost and don't carry this foolishness a step further. There are other patrons waiting to be served."

I looked around and counted them—seven in all. Only three of them had been served. I took an instant dislike to the big, heavy-muscled, leather-jacketed type near the far end of the counter. His large-featured face had a rough-textured, almost leathery look and he was glaring at me as if Miss Enslow's delay in taking his order was entirely my fault—which, of course, it was.

There was such an impatient shifting about all along the counter that I almost failed to recognize Mr. Martin. He was sitting on the end stool, right next to the leather-jacketed type, with his face buried in a menu. He'd apparently entered the restaurant and made his way to the counter right after I'd looked around for the third time, and decided I'd made a mistake in thinking you could count on anyone—least of all Mr. Martin—to arrive at a certain place at a certain time. Behavior patterns that weren't human were bound to be erratic and my failure to take that into consideration had upset me so much that I'd made another mistake that was just as inexcusable.

52

The banter I'd exchanged with Miss Enslow had been harmless enough, but why had I gone on and given myself away so disastrously?

I watched her now as she leaned toward Mr. Martin to take his order. To my surprise he tossed the menu aside, shook his head and pointed to the coffee percolator. If all he wanted was a cup of coffee why had he wasted two full minutes studying the menu? Wasn't the food to his taste—or was coffee his only nutritional need and the menu inspection staged for my benefit?

Miss Enslow nodded, walked to the percolator and drew a cup of steaming hot coffee. A slight wisp of smoke arose from it as she set in down in front of him, and moved back in my direction to take another order.

What happened then was so startlingly out of character that it seemed almost deliberate, although I can't believe that it was. Mr. Martin, whose usual lack of nervousness was the one thing that might have betrayed him in a situation where absolute calmness would have provoked comment allowed his hand to tremble slightly as he raised the coffee cup to his lips.

It never reached his lips, but fell from his fingers instead and the scalding brew drenched the trousers of the leather-jacketed man.

There are men with minds so inflammable that an accident of that nature can produce a detonation of almost unimaginable violence, and the heavy-muscled near-giant leapt up cursing, gripped Mr. Martin by both shoulders and lifted him bodily from the stool.

He went reeling with him out into the middle of the restaurant and hurled him with a straining of his entire bulk toward the jukebox that stood against the opposite wall. Ordinarily nothing more than a shattering crash would have ensued, followed by the slow descent of a bruised and shaken Mr. Martin to the floor. But something quite different happened.

There *was* a shattering of glass, but Mr. Martin didn't sink to the floor. He went staggering backwards instead, with a long sliver of glass projecting from his chest. He was clutching at it and tugging, his body bent almost double, and his assailant was recoiling from him with a look of horror in his eyes before the last large fragment of glass fell with a crash from the completely shattered face of the machine.

Clearly the leather-jacketed man had not intended to commit so terrible an act of violence and the instant Miss Enslow screamed he turned, raced for the door and was gone.

I'll never forget the look on Mr. Martin's face when he finally succeeded in wrenching that foot-long glass bayonet from his chest and holding it out in his hand. In a searing, terrible way the sight became indelibly etched on my brain. There was a look of agonized incomprehension in his eyes, and he kept moving his free hand back and forth across his chest until his fingers contracted and remained in just one spot, as if to stanch a flow of blood.

Three men leapt up, and started toward him across the floor, but he straightened abruptly and waved them back.

"I'm all right," he said, his voice surprisingly firm and loud. "Quite all right. It went through my wallet and barely grazed my flesh. Please—let's not send for the police and make something out of this that will get into the papers. I'm sure the restaurant wouldn't want that. I know the proprietor quite well—"

It was so strange and unheard of a request that no one seemed to have anything to say in reply. They just continued to stare at him in stunned disbelief and made no attempt to prevent him from bending, setting the glass bayonet down on the floor and drawing himself up again to his full height.

In all that time he hadn't even looked in my direction. As he walked toward the door he stopped only once, to lean across the counter and whisper something to Miss Enslow. Then he went through the door and I could see him for a moment through the window, walking on the sunny side of the street with an assured and measured stride, his shoulders squared.

5 LAURA HARTLEY

THE MOST moving and revealing aspects of human experience are often fugitive in nature, so that they are barely perceived by the conscious mind before they vanish, like ripples on a calm sea briefly set in motion by the wind, or a leaf spiraling skyward to be quickly lost in the immensity of the sky.

Perhaps that is why I became a librarian—not only because from the day I could toddle I have found myself irresistibly drawn to books, but because I like to guide others toward those fugitive revelations of beauty and wisdom which are just as often to be found between the pages of a great book as they are in the autumn woods or on a shining beach when the waves are cresting into foam.

Just to look out across the reading room on Saturday mornings, when it is crowded to capacity and at least a third of the readers are boys and girls in their middle 'teens is reward enough for a woman crowding thirty, who, in the eyes of those children, is verging on withered spinsterhood.

I particularly enjoyed watching Bobby Jackson, the library's only really shining adornment in what, for me, was a difficult-to-reason-with and occasionally infuriating age group.

As a rule, boys under fifteen are supposed to remain upstairs in the children's reading room. But at the age of twelve Bobby had succeeded in talking me into making an exception in his case.

I've never regretted having given him a temporary adult-privilege slip—I might as well have stamped "permanent" on it, since we both knew it was unlikely to be revoked—for just watching his eyes light up when he encountered something new and wonderful in the pages of a book made me feel as if I were slowly turning about in my hand a golden nugget that we'd mined together.

I always knew when he had one of those sudden glimpses of truth or beauty that come and go in a flash, and the exciting possibility that his entire future might be influenced by something he'd read in a library over which I had sole dominion made me feel very proud.

Occasionally I'd go up to him and put my arm around his shoulder and ask: "How are we making out this morning, Bobby?" and he'd say something in reply that would make that shared discovery feeling seem even more pronounced.

This Saturday morning there was nothing about the reading room that struck me as unusual—except that Bobby had become so absorbed in the book he was leafing through that he failed to even look up when I crossed the room to the window and half lowered the shade.

On the way back to the desk I stopped, and said: "You should never read when the sunlight is right on the book that way, Bobby. You'll ruin your eyes."

"I knew you'd lower the shade," he said.

"Oh?" I said. "You take a great deal for granted, Bobby. If I hadn't been looking in your direction—"

"You'd have gotten up and lowered the shade anyway," he said.

Unexplained mysteries, even small ones, have a way of cutting down my efficiency when I have to go through the tedious, never-ending process of slipping library cards in and out under the photo-duplicating machine and what Bobby had said made me determined to make him explain himself right then and there.

"How did you know?" I asked.

"It was easy," he said, and I had the feeling he was hardly aware I'd asked the question and was still nine-tenths absorbed in what he was reading.

I didn't like that kind of an answer.

"I asked you how you knew," I said, sharply. "Not how easy it was. Surely you can't read my mind, Bobby!"

"If I wanted to," he said.

"If you wanted—"

"Sunlight . . . getting in my eyes," he mumbled impatiently, as if wishing I'd go away. "I told you to—"

Suddenly he straightened, put down the book and looked at me as if he were seeing me for the first time that morning. His shoulders jerked and a slow flush crept up over his face.

"I—I'm sorry, Miss Hartley," he stammered. "I hardly heard what you were saying."

He'd heard, all right. I was sure of that. But sometimes you can be so preoccupied questions just don't register the way they should. I've had that experience often enough. Usually there's nothing illogical about what you say in reply. But all you're really trying to do is to eliminate a kind of static interference deep in your mind, and you tune it out unconsciously, without realizing you may have said something you never actually intended to blurt out.

"You expected me to lower the shade because you told me to," I said. "That's what you started to say and

57

I'm holding you to it. It makes no sense at all to me. But that doesn't alter one syllable of it."

There were ten adults and three teen-agers in the reading room and now they were all staring at us. I was keeping my voice lowered. But that couldn't excuse the worst crime a librarian can commit—breaking her own, sternly insisted upon rule of silence.

"I—I didn't mean it that way," Bobby said. "I was just hoping you'd lower the shade and I knew you would —if I got up and asked you. So I didn't feel I had to get up. It's like—well, sometimes when you're sitting in a crowded bus and you stare very hard at the passenger in front of you . . . he'll turn around and look at you. People seem to know—"

"So you were just conducting a little experiment in extrasensory perception," I said.

"If you want to call it that," he said. "I'm not sure I would. It's so attenuated."

Attenuated! Trust Bobby to use an expression like that. Clouding the issue by dragging in a completely irrelevant qualification. If you can get someone to do something just by staring at him you've communicated with him telepathically. There was, of course, a modicum of half-truth in what Bobby had said. It's so simple an experiment that most people have tried it at one time or another and have been amazed by how often it seems to work.

Telepathy on that level is more or less taken for granted. But what Bobby failed to realize was that he was using something no one could prove to try to convince me that I should dismiss his carrying telepathy a step further as equally inconsequential.

I don't know why I'd let myself become so upset by what Bobby seemed to think he'd done. It was silly, it made no sense at all, and I wasn't really angry at him. But I hate to have someone make a positive statement

58

and then try to squirm out of it as Bobby had done.

"You said you *told* me to cross the room and lower the shade," I persisted. "It wasn't just something you hoped I'd do, apparently, in response to a vague mental nudge on your part."

Before he could reply a voice that made me jump—even though I recognized it—whispered close to my ear: "You're setting a bad example, Goddess. Silence may not always be golden. But here it is presumed to be sacred, and for the presiding deity herself to so grievously offend—"

Every time John Dyson talked like that I regretted that there was no bucket of ice water within reach that I could, by standing on tiptoe, overturn on his head.

I was no more angry at him than I was at Bobby Jackson. But what can you do when someone you like persists in assuming that you're always in a carefree, socially irresponsible mood and can be whirled around and around on a dance floor that exists only in his mind? And what right had he to startle me half out of my wits by crossing the reading room on rubber soles and slipping one arm about my waist, completely ignoring what one of his own pupils might think.

He took his arm away quickly enough when I stiffened in reproach, but not before everyone in the reading room had time to be shocked by the outrageousness of it.

If I'd seen him enter the library I'd have taken care to remain at the desk, and no telepathic command on Bobby's part could have made me get to my feet. Sitting down, with the desk between us, I'd have been reasonably safe, even though he has a long reach.

Now the harm was done, and I was quite sure that the three elderly gossip-spreaders at the next table—Miss Hargrave was the worst—had no doubt at all that there was a "thing" between us. I wouldn't have minded so much if it had been true. When there is more truth than

59

falsehood in what is being said about you there is nothing to prevent you from summoning a fine spirit of independence to your aid. You have the right to insist that your private life is your own affair, and stand your ground with defiant banners unfurled. But when the whispering is a complete lie defiance and independence wither on the vine. How can you defend yourself against something you wouldn't feel guilty about if it were the opposite of false? You can, of course, but not with conviction. The only thing that angers you then is just the maliciousness of the gossip itself and the will to do battle is correspondingly weakened.

By tonight, I told myself, it would be all over town. In fairness to John Dyson—I'm quite sure he had no idea that just by putting his arm lightly about my waist and removing it quickly he had given gossiping tongues an opportunity to wag. Practically all men have moments of small-boy impulsiveness and irresponsibility. But he could have taken a lesson from Bobby Jackson.

At the age of fourteen Bobby could have set his thirty-two year old mentor a shining example in self-containment. He was doing so now, pretending to find in the book he'd been reading a passage so interesting that he was unable to tear his gaze from the page.

"Hello, Bobby" John Dyson said, as if noticing him for the first time. It was a neglect which a star pupil had every right to resent. But all Bobby did was look up quickly and grin at him.

"Miss Hartley and I have been discussing extrasensory perception," he said. "I guess there must be something in it . . . because other people seem to know exactly what you're thinking at times."

I wasn't sure, but it seemed to me that a startled look came into John Dyson's eyes.

"That's interesting, Bobby," he said. "What made you—"

I cut him short by laying a firm hand on his arm. "We've done enough whispering. You just said I was setting a bad example."

"I also said that a goddess was privileged," he reminded me. "Even if you weren't a goddess the privilege would still exist. In the ancient world, at the shrine of Apollo, the oracle was always a woman, and she was privileged to talk as much as she pleased. And since you're the sacred custodian here, as well as a goddess—"

"I'm not a goddess and I'm not privileged," I snapped. "I'm ashamed of myself—and I should think that you'd be. There is some excuse for Bobby, because I encouraged him to talk."

I was speaking only half-seriously, of course, and he was being the opposite of serious. But that didn't mean I wasn't also inwardly disturbed and a little angry. Incongruities always upset me, and it seemed a strange way for John Dyson to talk in Bobby's presence. How could Bobby respect the reading room rule of silence if a teacher took it so lightly that he could jest about it in so beguiling a way that, for an instant, I had shared his lack of seriousness?

Did he think of Bobby as so different from his classmates that the decorum which a teacher is supposed to maintain even in his more unguarded moments could, without risk, be tossed completely aside? Had the distance which is supposed to separate a teacher from his pupils dwindled so astonishingly in respect to Bobby that it had ceased to act as a barrier to a shared and casual goodfellowship on a completely adult level?

What, I wondered a little wildly, could have given me such an idea? It had seemed to creep almost unbidden into my mind and it lingered for a moment as if reluctant to depart.

I turned abruptly and walked back to the desk, quite sure that the whispering had annoyed everyone in the

61

reading room, including a stranger—a Lakeview transient, no doubt—who had greeted me with a smile when I'd crossed the room to lower the shade. His face seemed vaguely familiar and quite possibly I'd seen it before. But I was sure of only one thing—the smile had turned into a glare.

John Dyson followed me to the desk. I sat down with the photo-duplicating machine between us, and pretended to busy myself with re-arranging the cards in a drawer I'd taken out of the gray-metal, A to H index cabinet before I'd made the mistake of engaging in a battle of words with Bobby Jackson.

That very foolish verbal exchange was still echoing in my mind, making me feel more self-conscious than I had the evening before when John Dyson had taken me into his arms and brought his lips down hard on mine, directly in front of a restored, fan-lighted Georgian-period door. A garden apartment with that kind of front door is hard to find in Lakeview, but right at that moment the architecture hadn't seemed to interest him at all.

He stood watching me thumb through the index cards in tight-lipped silence for a moment, then leaned abruptly forward and pushed the drawer aside.

"Whatever you and Bobby were discussing must have been most interesting," he said. "Why didn't you want to talk about it?"

"If you must know," I said. "I find it hard to forgive what you did a moment ago. It was inexcusable. You've made everyone think you didn't come here to read or take out a book."

"You're so right," he said. "They know now there's one man in Lakeview who doesn't think of you as just an extremely friendly librarian . . . a little on the mousey side. I can't imagine how anyone ever got that idea in the first place."

"Just because we've had dinner together a few times,"

I retorted, "you seem to feel that you've a perfect right to walk into the library and throw your arms around me whenever you have an impulse to make a spectacle of yourself. In an age as tumultuous as ours a friendly, old-fashioned librarian can make a man feel very grateful —but not *that* grateful. No one was deceived by it. You say you didn't want them to be, and I think I know why. It's flattering to your male ego to feel you've discovered something in me that no one else has noticed."

"Now look—"

"Did it ever occur to you," I went on relentlessly, "that whatever it is you think you've discovered may be non-existent? I *am* a little on the mousey side and no miraculous new hairdo could possibly disguise it."

"Now you're talking absolute nonsense," he said. "Whether you know it or not, you're an extraordinarily attractive woman. It's just that the dust on these shelves keeps swirling up around you, preventing people from seeing you clearly."

"The library is spotless and you know it," I said. "I'd lose my job in short order if I allowed dust to accumulate on the books, even though some of them are practically never taken out."

"Well . . . have it your own way," he said. "*I* happen to think you're beautiful. A true goddess, arising from the waves enveloped in seven mysteriously weaving veils."

How can you reason with someone who talks like that?

I made one more try. "I hope what happened last night hasn't made you feel the goddess has feet of clay," I said. "It was a goodnight kiss, nothing more. I was a little surprised when you seemed to take it so seriously."

"For me it was a kind of—well, blockbuster," he said. "It shattered all of my deeply ingrained shyness. And when once shyness is broken down and all of your defenses are leveled, so to speak, you often do foolishly

63

reckless things. That's why I'm asking you to forgive me for the way my arm went around you for an instant. I had no intention of embarrassing you."

"What an odd thing to say about a kiss!" I said. "A blockbuster. I thought kisses were supposed to be tender."

"We tried to keep it that way," he said. "But I'm not quite sure we succeeded."

"Now you're making me feel as if I should be the one to apologize," I said. "Perhaps we'd better just forget the whole thing."

"That would be impossible," he said. "You still haven't told me whether or not you forgive me."

"If you give me your solemn word it won't happen again."

"Never on Sunday—or during library hours," he said. "I promise."

I'm sure he knew, from the way I was looking at him, that he'd won a small victory. But he must have wanted to be absolutely convinced that it was likely to last, for he waited a full minute before he said: "Now perhaps you'll tell me why you were having an argument with Bobby Jackson about telepathy."

"He didn't say it was an argument—and neither did I," I reminded him. "He called it a discussion."

"Well, a discussion then."

"It happened to be an argument," I said. "The sun was shining in Bobby's eyes, so I got up and crossed the reading room to lower one of the windowshades. On my way back to the desk, I stopped at his table to warn him that he was ruining his eyes, and—well, he told me he'd known I'd lower the shade. I don't think he quite realized what he was saying; he was still too deeply absorbed in the book he was reading. I asked him *how* he'd known and his reply angered me a little."

"What did he say, Laura?" John Dyson asked. I looked at him in surprise, wondering why he'd interrupted me

64

so impatiently. Apparently what Bobby had said was of the utmost importance to him.

"He said he had *told me* to cross to the window and had known that I would . . . because he'd communicated with me telepathically. We fell to arguing about it, but not before he looked terribly startled, as if he'd let something slip out he hadn't intended to say."

"I see," John Dyson said, nodding. "I'm afraid there are many things about Bobby he's trying very hard to conceal—from almost everyone. I can't seem to get through to him completely and he likes and trusts me as much as he does his own family. That's saying a great deal, because he worships his father."

I was startled by the look of concern that had crept into John Dyson's eyes. His expression had become wholly serious, as if what he had been saying to me a moment before had emerged from a part of his mind across which a curtain had been drawn.

"I've known for some time that something is troubling Bobby," I said. "Did you think it would come as a complete surprise to me?"

He seemed relieved when I said that. "No, not too much of a surprise," he replied quickly. "You're very observant, and Bobby visits the library—how often? Three or four times a week?"

"At least that," I told him.

"And stays how long, as a rule?"

"Sometimes three or four hours," I said. "Especially on Saturday mornings."

"What kind of books does he read?" John Dyson asked.

"He used to read history, biography, works of general science and now and then a novel—Faulkner, Hemingway, Bellow. H. G. Wells, too—and Jules Verne. Poetry —Shelley, Baudelaire and Poe, of course. Nothing juvenile—not even *The Last of the Mohicans*. He thought Cooper had a childishly ridiculous style and once revised

65

three pages of the *Pathfinder* as an example of how it should have been written. If he had re-written the entire book I'm sure he would have improved it enormously. But that wouldn't have been too brilliant an accomplishment. I doubt if he could have improved a single paragraph in *Moby Dick* despite the oceanic roll of the sentences. Or Henry James, with his page-long sentences."

"And now?" John Dyson asked.

"For the past month or so just books about—" I hesitated.

"About what, Laura?"

"You might call them non-fiction science novels," I said. "We have perhaps fifty or sixty books that fall into that general category, all of them fairly recent. They're novel-like in the sense that they're highly imaginative and build up to a kind of dramatic climax. They don't even pretend to be straight-line scientific treatises. They speculate imaginatively about what might happen *if*. *If* the world came to an end tomorrow or in the near future—or someone made a mistake and pressed the wrong button at Cape Kennedy. But they're non-fiction-like in having no plot structure, or character conflict—no drawing together of the threads. They adhere, for the most part, to just one rigidly established premise throughout."

"Could you cite, off-hand, a few of the titles?" he asked.

"Well . . . *ARE WE ALONE IN THE UNIVERSE OF STARS, THE COSMIC DISTANCE FACTOR RE-EX-AMINED, MULTIDIMENSIONAL UNIVERSES, SPACE TRAVEL BEYOND THE SPEED OF LIGHT, THE SILENT WATCHERS, UFO'S AND THE TEM-PORARY BASE HYPOTHESIS, TANGENTIAL SPACE AND THE INHABITANTS OF OTHER WORLDS, STRANGE PHYSICAL CHANGES IN EARTH'S OUTER ATMOSPHERE.* Very few of them

66

bear the imprint of major publishers and none of them have been widely reviewed."

"He draws out quite a few books too, doesn't he?" John Dyson asked.

"Oh, yes," I replied. "Seven or eight a week. Just in the past fortnight he's worked his way through all of the titles that interested him the most. He's on one of them now."

I glanced across the reading room partition to where Bobby was sitting with his eyes glued to *MESSAGES FROM SPACE—FACT OR FANTASY?* I had the feeling that he'd been looking straight at me and had lowered his eyes just in time to avoid giving himself away. If he could read my thoughts—which I refused to believe—he could hardly have failed to feel that I had just committed an act of betrayal. A small, not too grievous one, perhaps, but still—

I've always believed that for a librarian to reveal to an inquisitive stranger the titles of the books a borrower may choose to draw out is almost as bad as a tattletale breach of professional ethics by a lawyer or physician. But John Dyson wasn't a stranger and we were both equally concerned about Bobby's welfare—which may or may not have excused it.

6 LAURA HARTLEY

MY FEELING of guilt increased when John Dyson said: "He must have finished and returned quite a few of those books. I wonder if I could have a look at three or four of them."

"But why?" I asked, feeling somehow that Bobby's eyes were on me again.

"Something is seriously troubling Bobby," he said. "You've sensed it yourself. He's changed greatly, just in the past two or three weeks. The books may give us a clue as to precisely what is causing it. In a boy his age it's not too difficult to nip in the bud a quirk of thinking or feeling that could lead to a serious psychological stumbling block to his ability to adjust, in a healthy, normal way, to what's ahead of him. He's just on the threshold of adolescence now, and the next three or four years are certain to be critical ones. Between fourteen and eighteen a slight twist in the guidelines can send even a brilliant youngster spinning out over the abyss."

Even though I knew he was speaking metaphorically there flashed into my mind a picture of Bobby dangling from a high peak in the Swiss Alps, the rope just about to part, the climbers above, all adults, looking down appalled, powerless to be of any help. And Bobby looking up, just as appalled, his eyes widening as he saw that the abyss which yawned beneath him had begun to darken, changing from misty blue to an all-engulfing blackness.

"We may be completely mistaken about him," I said. "It may be just a phase he's passing through, no more important than what usually happens when a boy his age comes down with measles or the mumps, and has to stay indoors over the Fourth of July. The disappointment usually takes at least a fortnight to wear off."

"Bobby hasn't had any disappointments of that kind," John Dyson said. "He hasn't missed a day of school this year. It goes deeper than that."

"And you expect to find out what it is just by looking

68

at the books he's read and returned?" I persisted. "How can that give you even an inkling—"

"He may have made some marginal notations," John Dyson said. "He makes comments in pencil on some of his schoolbooks. In fact, the ones he turned in last term were so scrawled up that if he hadn't been Bobby Jackson I would have reprimanded him severely."

I was as shocked as only a librarian can be by so heinous a transgression.

"He'd never mark up library books!" I protested. "Not Bobby."

"Why not Bobby?" he asked. "College presidents have been known to do it. Sometimes the urge to talk back to some dolt of an author becomes irresistible and I bet you've erased a good many marginal notations when they've been called to your attention."

It was true, of course. But it always makes me indignant, and somehow it was hard for me to picture Bobby deliberately defacing public property.

Still . . .

"All right," I said. "We'll see."

Without glancing again in the direction of the reading room I got up and crossed the library to Sections C, D, and E. I walked up and down through the aisles, collecting four books that Bobby had returned earlier in the week. I had to open two of them and check the replacement cards, since I couldn't remember all of the titles he'd taken out. I was almost certain I wouldn't find any penciled comments if I flipped through the pages, since if Bobby had the annotation habit it would have come to my attention during the weeks which had elapsed since his reading room privilege had been widened to include the actual borrowing of downstairs books.

Despite what John Dyson had said about Bobby's schoolbooks I happened to know he handled library books with care—was, indeed, almost over scrupulous in that respect.

People will make marginal notes, though, as John Dyson had reminded me, and it certainly wasn't to be compared with such acts of vandalism as tearing the illustrations from a book, or turning down the corners of every third or fourth page.

What if the marginal comments were very brilliant, I wondered . . . better than anything else in the book? In that case would a librarian be justified in erasing them, and spoiling the pleasure which the next reader might derive from them? Wasn't it even possible that more than one unknown writer of genius had achieved creative fulfillment simply by annotating the pages of library books?

I stood very still, holding the four books in the crook of my arm, wondering what could have put such an absurd notion into my head. Why had I picked that particular moment to ask myself a question I ordinarily wouldn't even have entertained. My duty as a librarian was very clear in that respect, and there was no need for me to make a mountain out of a non-existent molehill.

It seemed incredible to me that such a thought could have come into my mind at all when I'd simply gone to the shelves to get four books which John Dyson seemed to feel might be of value in shedding light on what was troubling his most brilliant pupil.

No matter how much scribbling Bobby had or hadn't done on the margins it wasn't necessary for me to find excuses for him by defending the practice as genius-inspired. Quite possibly Bobby had felt that way about it, but as far as I was concerned—

For an instant I couldn't seem to breathe. *Bobby might have felt that way about it!*

Were the thoughts that had come trooping into my mind not really my thoughts at all? Or were they my thoughts wheeling about in stiff military formation under Bobby's command and marching off into an unexplored wilderness where the minds of a grown woman and a fourteen-year-old boy could communicate and wage a kind of friendly-unfriendly warfare? There is an inescapable antagonism that the young always harbor toward their elders, no matter how well-meaning their intentions may be, and what if Bobby—

I put the thought resolutely from me. When you're asked to do something absurd—and John Dyson's request made very little sense—the mind has a perfectly natural tendency to wander off into byways equally absurd, solely to keep self-recriminations at bay.

A great deal could be said for marginal notations. Didn't the libraries of the world's great often contain hundreds of such penciled jottings, so that when the books were put up for auction after the owner's death the bidding skyrocketed—particularly when some ill-deserved literary reputation was completely demolished by some brilliantly incisive comment that was a classic of its kind?

It was then that actual words seemed to echo through the corridors of my mind in a voice that could not have been my own. "Genius is always privileged to make its own rules . . . in a great many areas of human experience. One should be grateful that the rules are not set aside more often, since so many of them make no sense at all."

I looked down and saw that my right hand was trembling. But sometimes just the weight of four large books can produce such a tremor, and I tightened my lips and walked swiftly back to the desk, where John Dyson was tapping impatiently with his fingers on the base of the photo-duplicating machine.

"All right," I said. "Here they are. I hope Bobby doesn't get up and come to the desk while you're examin-

71

ing them. It's an irreverent kind of prying . . . if you want my honest opinion."

"You don't really think that," he said. "We're both trying to help Bobby overcome an emotional quirk . . . so that he can grow up as straight and resilient as a young willow tree."

Whenever he stopped being serious and talked like that—I've mentioned this before and it weighs on me heavily—I round it very difficult to forgive him. But I always did—and regretted it afterwards.

I've often wondered why most men prefer to have a woman help them when they undertake a foolish task? Do they have a guilt feeling they think can be lessened if they secure the tacit approval of the more sensible sex in that sly, underhanded way?

I felt that he was making me a fellow-conspirator when he handed me two of the books and said: "Suppose you go through these while I check on the other two."

I was on the point of telling him to complete the task alone, that I wasn't going to conspire any further against Bobby just to please him. Then I remembered the strange thoughts that had come trooping into my mind, and even though I still refused to believe that Bobby could have been responsible for them I found myself becoming a little angry.

It was wholly irrational. But since John Dyson was giving me a feeling of guilt anyway I decided I might as well stop being self-critical and confirm what I was almost sure of—that I wouldn't find a marginal comment anywhere in the two books.

I found the first completely unmarked and was slowly turning the pages of the second, *ARE WE ALONE IN THE UNIVERSE OF STARS?* When I caught my breath and darted a swift glance at John Dyson, hoping he hadn't noticed that I'd straightened in sudden startlement.

He hadn't, apparently. He was still turning the pages

of the largest of the four books, *MULTIDIMENSIONAL UNIVERSES,* his brow furrowed in thought.

The marginal comment was very brief and in Bobby's boyish, not too accomplished handwriting, which ruled out the possibility that it had been made by some other reader.

High up on the page, directly opposite an underlined paragraph Bobby had written: *Clairvoyance? Of course. He must have known . . . as I know.*

The underlined paragraph I read very quickly, my heart skipping a beat.

*And what if they appeared in our midst as they really are, creatures so alien that we would be instantly forewarned? Would a highly intelligent race commit so incredible an act of folly? Hardly. One can be sure, however, that they would lose no time in putting their inscrutable endowments to work in other ways . . . and there is one that could prove disastrous on a worldwide scale. How hard would it be for such a race to counterfeit the genuine coin of our common humanity, which unites us all even when we are most at odds? If we were asked to choose between a social or political enemy and an enemy that is unknown and faceless or hideous beyond belief can there by any doubt as to what our choice would be? The human voice alone inspires confidence, and the features and gestures of a fellow human being could be a weapon for our undoing. Who would suspect, who could know, that a friendly neighbor —or even a foe with nothing particularly terrifying about him, and inspiring much the same kind of confidence—*MIGHT NOT BE HUMAN AT ALL!

I hadn't gone far astray, I decided, in describing the books Bobby had recently displayed such an interest in as nonfiction science novels. This one was no different from the few I had read—a kind of Rorschach test wild excursion into the unknown. The author was comparatively unknown and had died a few months after the volume's arrival at the library. The index card listed no other titles beneath his name and a brief summary of what the book was about. Referring back to the card would have provided me with no additional information, for I had typed out the summary myself, and could remember it word for word. It was simply a condensation of the blurb which had appeared on the jacket and although the jacket had been removed I was quite sure that I'd left out nothing of importance.

Despite the author's obscurity the book had apparently fascinated a great many readers, for it had been drawn out fifteen times in six months.

That it had fascinated Bobby Jackson seemed indisputable. But just what did his strange comment mean. *He must have known . . . as I know.*

Known what? That there would be nothing monsterlike about the inhabitants of another world if they should decide to invade and conquer the Earth? No—that wasn't it, exactly. They *would* be monsterlike but no one on Earth would know because they would look like—friendly neighbors? The man or woman next door? I decided I couldn't be sure exactly what the author had in mind unless I read the entire chapter, and I certainly couldn't do that when at any moment John Dyson might glance up from *MULTI-DIMENSIONAL UNIVERSES* and catch me looking startled.

Should I protect Bobby or not? What if John Dyson was right and he was in danger of becoming emotionally disturbed at an age when the trend could only be reversed by winning his confidence and making sure that intelligent adult guidance would be on hand whenever he had need of it?

74

He must have known . . . as I know. Surely no experienced child psychologist would have failed to recognize in such a comment, brief as it was, an alarming indication that all was not well with Bobby.

Up to the age of eight or ten children often have ideas about themselves which, in an adult, would be diagnosed as paranoid. But Bobby was too old for that kind of illusion-creating self-deception. What was basically playacting in a very young child could be serious indeed in a boy of fourteen, for he would be aware of what a strain he was placing on credulity by claiming that, in some mysterious way, he had stumbled on a secret which no one else—except perhaps the author of *ARE WE ALONE IN THE UNIVERSE OF STARS?*—could share with him.

I made up my mind very quickly. John Dyson would have to be shown the marginal comment and the underlined paragraph or I would be failing Bobby instead of protecting him.

John Dyson's concern, I now realized, had been fully justified. He hadn't been guilty of prying without reason into Bobby's choice of reading matter, and I owed him an apology for thinking that he had.

It happened so suddenly I was taken completely by surprise. I was just about to reach out, with my thumb in the book, and tap John Dyson on the shoulder when my fingers began to tingle. I thought at first it was just a neuralgic twinge—a not unusual occurrence when I've been thumbing through index cards for an hour or more —and I waited for it to go away.

It didn't. A violent shock went through my arm instead, from my fingertips to my elbow. It was like an electric charge, sudden, agonizing and in dismay I dropped the book and cried out.

The agony vanished the instant the book left my hand and when John Dyson turned and stared at me in con-

75

cern I found that I could move my fingers freely without bringing the pain back.

When he saw that I was rubbing my fingers to make sure he grinned at me.

"Oh, no!" he said. "Not rheumatism at your age."

I was too stunned to say anything in reply. I watched him as he bent and picked up the book, wondering what he'd think if I told him the truth.

I decided not to. There was no way of explaining it, and if he thought it was rheumatism well and good. You can have it at twenty and it's no disgrace.

The disgrace was in letting myself think what I did—that someone had not wanted me to call what Bobby had written on page sixty-seven of *ARE WE ALONE IN THE UNIVERSE OF STARS?* to John Dyson's attention.

To my amazement he flipped through the pages rapidly, a look of bitter disappointment on his face, and handed the volume back to me.

"Well, I guess I was mistaken," he said. "Bobby doesn't make marginal notes on library books. Schoolbooks are apparently less sacrosanct to him."

"But he does!" It was on the tip of my tongue to protest. "He—"

My throat began to tighten up and a wave of dizziness swept over me. I couldn't seem to get the words out and I had the feeling that if I tried too hard I'd be very likely to black out.

The dizziness lasted only a moment, but long enough for me to hear John Dyson say: "I'll call for you at a quarter to seven. The first show starts at eight-thirty and that should give us time to have dinner and get there a little ahead of the crowd." Just long enough for me to be aware that he had turned and was crossing the library to the reading room without a backward glance. I saw him stop, lay his hand on Bobby's shoulder and

76

talk to him for a moment. Then he crossed to the door, paused for an instant to smile and wave at me and descended the steps to the street. Through the window I could see him crossing Elm Street, hatless, his hair ruffled by the wind. He was weaving in and out between the traffic with his usual recklessness, ignoring the red *Don't Walk* light on the opposite curb.

The instant the dizziness passed I stared across the reading room partition again, and saw that Bobby had stopped reading. He was looking straight at me and there was an unmistakable look of triumph on his face.

After a moment he lowered his eyes, and I thought for an instant that he intended to go right on reading. But he closed *MESSAGES FROM SPACE—FACT OR FANTASY?* instead, got up and walked toward me with the book in his hand. He laid it down on the desk directly in front of me and smiled. There wasn't a trace of guilt or even embarrassed self-consciousness in his eyes.

"I may want to take this out later," he said. "I've read most of it, and I took two books out Thursday I may as well finish first."

I don't know what prevented me from gripping him firmly by the wrist and demanding to know if the books he read at home contained marginal notes so incriminating that his parents were in constant danger of being electrocuted. Possibly what prevented that kind of confrontation was the way he looked at me when I found that I could no longer control the trembling of my hands. They shook so when I picked up the book he must have realized that whatever I might say to him would jeopardize our friendship, and his eyes said as plain as words: "Try to forgive me. It was something I had to do."

He smiled again, turned abruptly and was gone. I saw him pass through the front door but he didn't cross Elm Street as his mentor had done. That didn't surprise me in the least, however. If he walked straight north and

77

kept on the shady side of the street he'd get home just as quickly, and people who are weighed down with guilt, no matter how young they are, have a tendency to shun the sunlight.

I should have gotten up, as soon as my hands stopped trembling and put back the book Bobby had returned. But for a full minute I couldn't seem to move, and I think now it was my utter stillness that made the stranger who was sitting by the reading room window decide that I would be unlikely to glance in his direction while he did something so unbelieveable that it made what Bobby had done seem merely to border on the strange.

The young man sitting by the window took his face apart!

It was done so quickly that the fingers of his raised right hand seemed scarcely to move. But as I stared toward the window, so appalled that a cold constriction began to tighten about my heart, I could see the flesh of his face being drawn away from his cheekbones, and a moist glistening where his eye-sockets had become as cavernous as the holes in a skull.

It could not have taken him more than ten seconds to reshape his entire face, using a doughy mass of stripped-away flesh to lengthen his nose, widen the contours of his jaw and give himself the features of a much older man.

If the eyes of the other readers had been on him as mine were at precisely that instant they would have seen the gruesome transformation taking place. But half of them had their backs turned to him, and the others were absorbed in their reading. He had evidently chosen the moment with care, making sure in advance that he would have eight or ten seconds grace, completely secure from observation. How could he have known I would raise my eyes so abruptly and look straight at him, witnessing, in the briefest of instants snatched from time's passing, a human-featured mask that cloaked something monstrous being taken apart and reshaped? How could he have considered it even a risk, when I had been sitting so still an instant before with my eyes riveted on the book which Bobby had returned to me?

Just as terrifying were the words that formed in my mind as I returned his coldly hostile stare: "I did not want the banker's son to recognize me. He has suspected the truth for some time, and I have been keeping him under constant observation. Now you *know* . . . and that is worse . . . much worse . . . much more of a danger. I am afraid that I will have to kill you."

7 BRUCE CONLEY

I HAD A feeling I'd like Lakeview the instant I descended from the train and looked around me. A half hour later I was sure of it. The town had sparkle, atmosphere. It had practically everything a town needs to sell itself to a live operator in the mechanical toy line, with a suitcase full of samples.

It wasn't large and it wasn't small—just a medium-sized rural community with two large smokestakes in the background to give it an up-and-coming industrial look. I wasn't selling anything a factory could use, but big smokestacks spell out progress to me and the prospect of a quick turnover.

There was a main shopping and business section branching off at right angles to a big, graystone building that

79

had "Town Hall" written all over it, and the main street was lined with stores, bars and attractive-looking restaurants sandwiched in between four-storey office buildings.

I had no idea where I'd find the prettiest waitresses, because that depends partly on blind luck and partly on how many middle-aged married men there are in the residential streets branching off from the restaurant you happen to pick.

The one I picked had a menu Scotch-taped to the window and the seafood specials appealed to me and the price was right. It was a kind of luncheonette but there were tables as well as a counter inside and I thought I could see just one waitress moving about between the tables. But it was hard to be sure from the street. It was a sizzling September day and the sun was right overhead, setting up a glare that made me wish I hadn't packed my smoked glasses where I couldn't get at them until I checked in at a hotel.

At that particular moment—I'd have settled for food alone, because I'd worked up an appetite that would have made me feel frustrated if I'd had to settle for a woman alone. A woman who's alone can usually make me postpone eating until I've convinced her there's no need for her to feel isolated and cut off from male companionship. But not this time. I was hungry enough to eat the candied grasshoppers food delicacy stores import from Japan for the man who has tried everything.

Besides, three or four waitresses were better than one *only* if the one failed to be special. The law of averages might be against it, but I've never trusted the law of averages too much, and what was to prevent me from walking straight into the restaurant and trusting to luck that she'd have a cute hairdo, and trim ankles and other pulse-stirring attributes to go with them I'd be certain to like?

I glanced once more at the menu, picked up my suitcase and with the kind of assured and easy stride that most women like and I don't have to put on—it just happens to be my natural way of walking when I'm not hurrying to catch a train—walked into the restaurant with my shoulders held straight.

Three seconds later I was setting the suitcase down again, so jolted by what I saw that I almost tripped over it in getting to her before she collapsed.

She was no longer moving about between the tables. She must have been staggering from the instant I'd first set eyes on her through the windowpane, because no woman could have looked the way she did without staggering.

Her expression was ghastly. She didn't seem to have any color at all in her face and her eyes were wide with fright and she was staring at one of the empty tables as if she feared it might suddenly come to life and move toward her on stalklike legs like a giant daddy-long-legs.

I had to put my right arm around her waist to steady her and keep her from collapsing. Just gripping her firmly by the arm wouldn't have kept her from sagging. I was sure of that and I was equally sure that she'd be grateful and not consider that I was stepping out of line.

I'd guessed right about one thing. She *was* special. Auburn-haired and blue-eyed and everything the kind of lad I was could really go for in a woman.

"What's wrong?" I said. "Suppose you just try to calm down a little and tell me. Talking usually helps. . . ."

"She—she was sitting right over there," she choked. "And he came up behind her and put his arms around her. She tried to get up from the table, but he wouldn't let her. He clamped his hand over her mouth to keep her from screaming. I saw him clearly for a minute, but I didn't see him come into the restaurant. He was just—

81

there. All at once, as if he'd stepped right out of the wall behind the table."

She was trembling violently now. "A middle-aged man with gray hair who has lunch here three days a week. He's well-dressed and has a nice face. I don't know his name. He usually sits at the counter, because he never comes in as early as this and when he's here the tables are roped off. A few days ago we thought we'd have to send for the police. Another man—I think he was a truck driver and drunk—got into a fight with him, and we thought for a minute he was seriously hurt. But he wasn't, and he kept me from phoning for the police by telling me he knew the proprietor. He said he was sure Mr. Winstock—it's Mr. Winstock's wife who owns the restaurant—wouldn't want any trouble, that it would give the restaurant a black eye. I found out later he didn't know Mr. Winstock at all."

"All that, you say, happened a few days ago?"

She nodded and leaned so heavily against me that I thought it advisable to tighten my hold on her waist.

"You think it had something to do with what happened just now?" I asked.

"No—I don't think so," she said. "That was just a fight with another man. Although—"

She hesitated, then went on quickly. "The jukebox was smashed and a splinter of glass seemed to go deep into his chest. But he pulled it out and there was no blood on the glass. But even that wasn't—"

Her voice failed her for a moment and she clung to me, still shuddering.

"You say a woman was sitting at that table and he came up behind her and prevented her from screaming," I said. "All right. Now suppose we take it from there. He must have frightened her, or she wouldn't have struggled and tried to get up from the table. What happened then?"

82

"She just looked at me as if she was desperately hoping I'd find some way to help her, but didn't really think I could. Then—the whole restaurant went dark for a minute, or seemed to, and—and—"

"Yes? Easy now."

"They were both gone!"

"Listen to me," I said. "You've had some kind of shock. You don't have to tell me about it all at once. We've got all the time in the world. They're not here now, so that means they must have both left a few minutes ago."

"No—no! It was less than five minutes ago, right before you walked in. And they didn't leave. Not in the way you mean. They just—vanished."

"You said it went dark . . . so you couldn't be sure of that," I reminded her. "How do you know they both just didn't get up and walk out of the restaurant?"

I caught myself up short. I was accepting what she'd told me without asking myself whether there was a grain of truth in her whole story. It was the wrong way of getting at the truth. When someone tells you something that's unbelievable you don't become as credulous as a six-year-old child straight off and go right along with it.

I reached out and drew a chair toward her and eased her down into it, regretting that it compelled me to relinquish my hold on her waist.

"Just who was sitting at that table?" I asked. "Did you know her?"

"Yes, of course. She dines here regularly. Miss Hartley, a librarian. I like her very much and we've talked a great deal, because we're both interested in the same things. I'll be getting my B.A. in the fall, and I'm seriously thinking of becoming a librarian."

Well—that was really something. Brains as well as beauty and enough spirit to take a waitress job in the summer to keep the board-and-tuition kettle boiling.

83

But right at the moment the way she still seemed to be collapsing, despite the supporting arms of the chair, made me too concerned to tell her how much I admired her independence of spirit.

"Now look," I said. "When you've had a bad shock you can't always be sure that what you think you've seen really happened. You must have heard of the little man who wasn't there. I'm not saying he wasn't there. I'm just saying he couldn't have walked out of the wall, put his arms around your librarian friend and dragged her back into the wall with him when everything seemed to grow dark."

"But he didn't carry her out of the restaurant," she protested, her voice so tremulous that it sharply increased my concern. "I was watching the door. It stayed light even when everything else seemed to grow dark. If he'd walked out into the street with her in his arms I'd have seen them."

I didn't tell her I'd been standing in front of the restaurant for at least three minutes studying the menu and trying to make up my mind whether she was special or not. I'd have seen him too—if it had all happened less than a minute before I'd decided to go in and find out. But I hadn't seen the restaurant grow dark either, so that evened it up.

I did something then I wouldn't have thought myself capable of, because it seemed so impulsively foolish and hard to justify—a spur-of-the-moment absurdity.

But perhaps it wasn't so foolish. She was obviously in a state of shock and in need of something to distract her attention.

I reached down, snapped open the heavy bag I'd carried with me into the restaurant and took out a little man. I set him down on the table in front of her. I didn't have to wind him up. All I had to do was flick a button.

84

He was just about the most ingenious mechanical toy ever built. He was wearing a tiny metal tuxedo, and there was a miniature carnation pinned to his lapel. You don't wear carnations with tuxedos, as a rule, but children don't mind that kind of make-believe. They take delight in it.

I flicked the button and the little man started walking. He walked completely across the table, swung about and walked solemnly back toward us again. And when he reached the end of the table and was directly in front of us he bowed—from the hips with a flourish of his right arm. Then he turned and started back across the table again.

I reached out and tapped her on the arm. "Shut your eyes," I said.

The instant she obeyed, with a look of utter astonishment on her face, I picked up the little man, bent and put him back in the suitcase again.

"Now you may look," I said.

She opened her eyes and stared at me. "He's gone! But of course. You put him back in that bag."

"How do you know for sure?" I asked. "You had your eyes closed for the barest instant."

"What are you trying to prove?" she demanded.

"Nothing at all," I said. "Except that that little man startled you and then—*whoosh,* he was gone. That increased your startlement. I could see that it did. When something startles you that much it's hard to be sure of anything."

"Well. . . ."

"I've half-convinced you already, haven't I? I can see it in your eyes. The worst mistake you could make would be to let what you thought you saw keep you awake nights, shivering."

Suddenly we were both laughing. "That's better," I said "How is the fillet of sole this morning?"

8 BOBBY JACKSON

I AWOKE from the worst nightmare I'd ever had. I'd spent
the afternoon fishing at the east end of the lake, and I
was walking home through the woods when I heard a voice
say: "Run, Bobby! Run for your life! They're all around
you but they can't see you yet. They have to bring you
into focus, and that's difficult, that takes time. Just start
running and don't look back. It's your only chance."

I'd turned then and started to run. But my legs started
getting heavy and soon I was moving so slowly I seemed
to be wading through a sea of glue.

"Bobby," the voice pleaded. "What's holding you up?
Aren't you the crazy one! All you have to do is run, but
you don't seem to want to save yourself."

"I can't!" I shouted back, which made no sense at
all, because the voice was coming from inside my head.
"Can't you see I'm bogged down?"

"Nonsense, Bobby. It isn't quicksand you're wading
through. Nothing like that at all. Make an effort, try. Do
you want them to catch you?"

There was a great, heavy silence in the woods now,
and it was worse than if there had been a shouting or a
screaming to urge me on. I felt suddenly as if everyone
I knew had deserted me, as if all the friends I once
had were standing at the stern of a ship that was moving off
through the woods on a launching slip, looking back at

me with cold reproach in their eyes because of something I hadn't done.

I started to run again then, and suddenly the heaviness was gone and I was weaving in and out between the trees like a wounded deer. I felt as if I were fleeing from a hundred hunters who had come swarming into the woods and torn down all of the *No Hunting or Fishing* signs to make sure they wouldn't get into trouble with the law before they started blasting away at me.

"Bobby, they're not deer hunters!" I heard the voice shouting again. "They're hunters of men and there is no closed season on that kind of sport."

"Who are they?" I shouted back. "I must know! Tell me!"

"Who knows, Bobby? They have traveled far and may come from other suns—yes, even from the Great Nebula in Andromeda! Don't let them catch you, Bobby. Run, *run!*"

"I can't keep it up much longer!" I shouted back. "I can hardly breathe now and my legs—"

Suddenly I couldn't see the forest for the trees. Each tree had grown larger and they were all bending down toward me with their branches interlocked and when I looked up all I could see was that cruel, dark web of vegetation descending.

I awoke drenched in cold sweat. Even my pajamas were drenched, and when I threw back the sheets and looked down over myself I thought for a minute. that my chest and legs were all covered with dark forest mould.

I blinked furiously and the terrifying illusion was gone. The sun was streaming into the room and I knew that it was another day and that I was still sound in body and mind.

Mom was knocking on the door, which was probably

what had awakened me. "Bobby," she called. "It's a quarter to eight. You'll be late again."

"What do you mean 'again', Mom?" I called back. "When have I ever been late for school?"

She opened the door and came into the room and stood looking at me without saying a word.

"What is it now?" I asked. "What have I done?"

"You catch me up on everything I say," she told me. "You're getting worse than your father in that respect. Your stubborn streak is getting worse too. When you sneeze all day long and I ask you to do something as simple as taking an aspirin you tell me you never had a cold in your life. When you—"

"Now Mom, please," I said. "I had a terrible dream and I don't feel like arguing. Just let me get dressed."

"You think I'm a terrible nag, don't you, Bobby?"

She sat down on the bed and slid her arm around me and held me tightly. "I'm not such a bad mother, am I, Bobby? Tell me honestly."

"Well . . ."

"I can't help getting impatient with you at times. You're so terribly stubborn."

"Well . . . perhaps you've got something there, Mom," I said.

"Admitting it makes you feel better, doesn't it? Why don't you do that more often? Then we wouldn't have any reason to quarrel."

"That's what I like most about you, Mom," I said. "You say 'quarrel' instead of 'speak harshly.' Don't think I don't appreciate it."

"I sometimes wonder if you really do."

She got up before I could reply and crossed to the door. "The oatmeal's on the stove and the coffee is beginning to perk," she said, her hand on the knob. "Don't take too long getting dressed. I'm glad you don't have to shave."

"It will happen soon enough," I said. "Then every morning the coffee is going to get cold. I'm meticulous about everything I do."

"By then you may be married and far away," she said. "I pity the girl—"

She went out and shut the door firmly behind her. She certainly wasn't the worst mother in the world and sometimes I thought she came pretty close to being the best.

But occasionally she made me so mad I'd get to feeling that all communication between us had broken down.

I don't like to just jump out of bed and put on the clothes I've draped over a chair the night before even when I'm a little late for breakfast. I prefer to go to the window first and breathe in the crisp September air, and look out across the lawn to see if I can spot a robin hopping about in search of a night-crawler—or some other bird that's rarely seen in Lakeview.

Bird watching isn't one of my major hobbies. But I've several notebooks full of jottings that would have earned me a pat on the back from the local chapter of the Audubon Society, if I hadn't let my membership lapse.

I usually spend above five minutes at the window, and then I go to the closet and look over my collection of sport shirts, and pick out one that I haven't worn for a week or so.

All of that takes time, of course, and I could picture Mom fuming and fretting while the cereal got cold and Dad annoyed her by going through the newspaper in tornado fashion, passing from the financial section to the sports page, and then to the news and not caring how much crinkling noise he made or even if half of the paper fell to the floor.

I decided to surprise her for once. There were no robins or other birds on the lawn, and the sport shirt I'd worn yesterday still had a freshly-laundered look. So I put it on, combed and brushed my hair, and was out of the room and descending the stairs five minutes after I'd crossed to the window.

There is no quick explanation as to why Mom serves buck wheat cakes about twice a month, along with oatmeal and scrambled eggs. But this was one of those mornings when the breakfast table should have made Dad happy, and it pained me a little to see that he wasn't surprising Mom at all. As usual, he had the morning paper propped up before him and there were two sections on the floor.

When he heard me approaching the table he thrust the paper aside, said: "Hello, son. A gorgeous morning, eh?" and started turning the pages again, probably to find out if the weatherman was going to let the sun go right on shining for the rest of the day.

Mom came out of the kitchen and set a pitcher of cream down in front of him. "Roger, you haven't too much time," she said.

I sat down and started in on the oatmeal, resenting the fact that I was just as much a slave to time as Dad was. What if I should be a few minutes late for school. Would Mr. Dyson give me a disciplinary lecture? Hardly. He'd take me aside and explain, not unreasonably, that while there were certain privileges attached to being a banker's son and a high I.Q. student I was creating a problem for him, because lateness, even on the junior executive level, didn't set well with the principal.

"You know how it is, Bobby. If I made an exception in your case I'd be in serious trouble."

You don't create problems for someone you like and respect and I'd have found myself right back where I started—a victim of the nine o'clock rush.

Dad was luckier. He didn't have to get to the bank before ten, but there was a bus he had to catch at nine-thirty if he wanted to avoid a thirty-five block walk, so Mom always lumped the difference in our time schedules and hurried us both along together.

Dad suddenly thrust the paper aside again and shook his head, glancing from Mom to me as if he'd read something that seemed unbelievable to him.

A surprised look appeared on Mom's face. Dad doesn't often get excited about news items and when he does it usually means that a new war has broken out somewhere, or a bank president, anxious to please, has let himself be talked into cashing a two-million-dollar rubber check.

"Anderson told me yesterday afternoon he was afraid this might get into the paper," Dad said. "I didn't think it would but apparently he was right. There unfortunately doesn't seem to be any way an officer of the law can stop a high-handed reporter from making him look like a fool."

"What is it, Dad?" I asked.

"A young man was picked up by Sheriff Anderson yesterday on Clarke Street who was absolutely convinced he had turned into a cat," Dad said.

For a moment the room tottered, and I couldn't seem to breathe.

"What's so unusual about that?" Mom asked, before Dad could go on. "If he was a mental case—"

"It's the Sheriff's story that's on the wild side," Dad said, shaking his head. "And Anderson is definitely not a mental case. I've known him for twenty years and I can't believe he'd lie to me about what he *thought* he saw. There must be some explanation for it . . ."

"What did he see, Dad?" I managed to get out.

"A cat that—for a brief moment, at least—seemed just as firmly convinced that it was a man," Dad said. "The whole thing—"

"Better give him the paper and let him read the story

91

for himself," Mom said. "He'll be late for school if you're going to make a TV documentary out of it."

Dad's temper rose at that. "When Bobby asks me a serious question I prefer to answer it in my own way," he said. "Do you mind?"

"Naturally I mind. But if you're determined to miss your bus, go right ahead."

"I can well afford to miss my bus two or three times a week," Dad said. "A two mile walk will do me good. I wish you'd stop *hurrying me out of the house!*"

Mom tightened her lips and returned to the kitchen without saying a word. On any other morning I'd have sided with Dad. But looking at the buckwheat cakes she'd baked just to please him I couldn't help feeling that he'd spoken much too harshly. I was still too shaken by what he'd just told me, however, to give that more than a passing thought.

I wanted him to go right on talking, because all you can ever get from cold print in a newspaper are facts seen through the eyes of just one reporter. Somehow they always seem to add up to a little less than the whole truth and nothing but the truth.

Dad had a rare gift for interpreting facts in an imaginative way. He didn't believe in keeping them in a deep freeze until they became stiff and brittle and as likely as not to break up into dozens of fragments. Just the fact that he'd talked to Sheriff Anderson in person and gotten his side of the story encouraged me to believe that if I was persistent and asked him just the right questions—and added my interpretation to his—we'd really get somewhere.

"Why was the young man arrested, Dad?" I asked. "Was he creating a disturbance?"

"First of all," Dad said, staring at the story as if he regretted he hadn't asked Mom for a pair of scissors, so that he could cut it out and show it to Mr. Graham and Mr. Creighton at the bank, "he was acting in a most peculiar way. It seems he'd stopped before a store window and was staring at his reflection in the glass. It must have frightened him in some way, because he kept backing away from it with his shoulders hunched. The Sheriff just happened to be passing. There was no one else at that time on that side of the street."

"What happened then, Dad?"

"People who have taken an oath to uphold the Law have a special responsibility," Dad said. "It's a kind of commitment. You or I—any ordinary citizen—seeing a young man behaving in that way—his name, incidentally, is Charles Bellamy—might not have attached much importance to it. But the Sheriff immediately became concerned. He went up to young Bellamy, and asked him what was wrong. Instead of replying Bellamy cringed back against the window and *hissed* at him."

"You mean—the way a cat would hiss?"

Dad looked at me as if surprised that I should have asked such a question. "Why yes . . . I suppose so," he said. "But anyone can make that kind of sound."

He was right, of course. It's as easy as whistling. You simply blow hard through your teeth and against the roof of your mouth. It's a distinct speech sound however, and the brain plays a part in producing it. In other words, you can't hiss or laugh or cry—unless instructions are flashed from the brain to the speech centers. But did that prove the young man thought that he had turned into a cat? Hardly. He could just as easily have been an act of deranged defiance and I knew there would have to be a great deal more to the story, or the News-Chronicle would never have printed it.

Dad seemed to feel that my question had been a trivial one—which, of course, it wasn't—and I could see that he was losing patience.

93

"Bobby," he said, suddenly. "I guess your mother was right. Here, read the story for yourself."

He started to pass me the paper, but I grabbed hold of his wrist and shook my head. "I watched you while you were reading it," I said. "It gave you quite a jolt, even though you talked with Anderson. If I read it I'd probably miss something that made you feel—I paraphrased what he'd said—it just about tops the list for wildness."

He looked at me and shook his head. "You're a very strange boy, Bobby," he said. "Sometimes it's hard for me to believe I'm your father. When you were six or seven I never could figure out why you'd give me a book to read—Hawthorne's *Twice Told Tales,* for instance—so that I could re-tell it in my own words as a bedtime story. I'm sure you missed some of the best things in the book that way."

"I liked what you added, Dad," I said. "I didn't feel that Hawthorne had any way of knowing how a twentieth century mind would feel about the golden legends of the ancient world. Not just how a boy of six would feel, but how an imaginative adult would feel. It sort of —well, added depth to the tales. Breadth as well. You saw things that I would have missed, and that Hawthorne left out. How could a writer born in 1804 take a century-long leap through time?"

"All right, all right," Dad said. "You've said enough. You scare me a little when you talk like that. You always have."

I knew exactly what he was thinking. *Maybe I've sired a precocious little efflander. A boy who should have been Merlin's son—with Einstein for a godfather.*

"You seem to forget I've just read this story," Dad said. "If your mother wasn't so impatient to start her day I could read the entire paper in leisurely fashion and separate the important items from the trash.

94

Nothing that you don't do thoroughly is worth the effort
—even to the reading of a newspaper."

Suddenly, to my surprise, Dad was grinning at me.
"That's what fathers used to say to their sons—back in
the Victorian Age. 'See how the busy little bee improves
each shining hour.' Unfortunately that kind of ridiculous
pontification hasn't died out completely. Fathers have
always been and always will be somewhat stuffy people,
I'm afraid. Not only in the eyes of the young, but in their
own eyes. Just having a son can make you forget at times
that there can be a lot of valuable and original ideas
knocking around inside a boy's head you'd do well to pay
attention to."

I doubt if I ever surprised Dad quite as much as he
occasionally surprised me. "Like father, like son," has a
solid core of truth to it. Genes are genes and you can't
get around them. If Dad hadn't been a little on the unusual
side where would I have been?

"When he hissed at the Sheriff what happened, Dad?"
I asked. "It must have given Mr. Anderson quite a jolt."

"Well . . . Anderson seemed to feel he was dealing with
a hundred percent whack," Dad replied, nodding. "He
reached out and grabbed hold of Bellamy's wrist and tried
to talk some sense into him."

Here it comes, I thought.

"And found he'd guessed right?" I asked, feeling a
certain dread rising in my mind. It wasn't easy for me
to forget how I'd felt in the old Oakham mansion, when
I'd seen Mrs. Parker's cat creeping across the floor and
had suddenly looked out upon the room through eyes
that were just as close to the floor and had even begun
to think and feel like a cat.

Sometimes you can wait impatiently for words you
know are almost certain to come and yet dread the moment when they will go crashing through your mind like a
tidal wave, leaving you without even a frail raft to cling to.

"About his being a whack, you mean?" Dad said. "Yes, Anderson certainly was justified in thinking that. He went right on hissing, and clawed and scratched and bit him twice on the wrist. Anderson rolled back his sleeve and showed me the toothmarks when we had our talk. He was like a wild animal, apparently."

A wild animal! Was that what I might have become if Helen Martin hadn't—

The room reeled again, and I missed a part of what Dad was saying. I was not at all ready to hear what I felt might be coming and was relieved when I heard him speaking words that were slightly reassuring.

"They questioned him later when he was locked up in a cell and had calmed down considerably. He answered every question Anderson asked him. He is twenty-five years old and lives with his widowed mother on Bretan Street. There was a reporter from the News-Chronicle at the jail and Anderson was so wrought up that he made the mistake of talking too much."

Dad paused an instant, then went on with a troubled look in his eyes. "Did you ever see a cat walking, Bobby?" he asked. "I mean—walking upright like a man and making frantic gestures with its forepaws? I certainly haven't, and what Anderson *thought* he saw may have been something quite different. He told me the cat darted out from behind a car parked at the curb and came toward him shaking its head from side to side. It stumbled once and seemed to be in a desperate hurry to get to him before Bellamy scratched his eyes out."

"How could he be *sure* the cat's movements were humanlike?" I said. "The difference in size between a cat and a man would make that very difficult to determine. Maybe the cat was simply darting about in a stiff, erratic way, as if it had collided with a live wire and been galvanized by the shock. There wouldn't have to be any

96

wire. Often cats leap about like that for no reason at all. They're strange animals."

"I know," Dad said, nodding. "That's a shrewd observation, Bobby, and it may just possibly have occurred to Anderson at first. But then the cat reached up and grabbed his hand between its forepaws and started to tug at it. Remember—I'm just telling you what he told me. It sank its claws in his wrist but not deep enough to draw blood and kept right on tugging. He says it was shaking all over. Its ears were flattened and it was making almost human sounds deep in its throat. He had the feeling it was trying to tell him something—God knows what."

"Probably to stop struggling with Bellamy, because there's nothing more dangerous than outside interference when something that unnatural is taking place," I said and could have bitten my tongue out.

Dad stared at me for an instant incredulously, as if he had hardly expected me to come to Anderson's defense. "You talk as if you really *believed* the Sheriff's story!" he said.

That was the last thing I wanted Dad to suspect. To keep him from coming too close to the truth I said quickly: "You told Mom you didn't think he was lying about what he *thought* he saw. If he was struggling with Bellamy and thought the cat was trying to get him to stop some pretty wild ideas must have flashed across his mind. It would have all seemed terrifyingly unnatural to him."

"That's true, of course," Dad conceded. "But he was a little vague at that point, probably because what happened next was even more unbelievable. Remember— I'm still just repeating what he said. He lost his head completely for a moment and kicked out at the cat, sent it careening across the pavement to the curb. He was genuinely frightened, as almost anyone would have been. The animal was clawing at his hand and beginning to

97

draw blood and he thought it was just crazed enough to be dangerous, particularly when he had to contend with a crazed human being as well.

"The kick took care of the cat. It screeched, righted itself and went darting across the street into a garage parking lot. The instant it vanished Bellamy stopped struggling. A dazed look came into his eyes and he stared at the Sheriff as if he were just awakening from a nightmare experience that had made him go berserk without being aware that he'd been behaving like a madman. His face twitched and he swayed back against the store window and covered his face with his hands. Anderson said his whole body shook and he muttered something very strange. "Outside my own body! Oh, God—how?"

I'd made the mistake of picking up a spoon and setting it down again, but Dad didn't seem to notice how my hand was trembling.

"Are you sure that's what he said, Dad?" I asked. "He didn't say anything else?"

Dad shook his head. "Not until later, when Anderson decided he'd made a mistake in arresting him and nothing was to be gained by keeping him locked up in a cell."

I could tell by the way Dad was frowning that Sheriff Anderson hadn't been very happy about whatever it was that Bellamy had told him.

But that didn't diminish my curiosity. "He must have had a lot of explaining to do," I said. "Did it make any sense?"

"He answered every question Anderson asked him," Dad said. "And it added up to—nothing at all."

"How could that be?" I asked.

"He resorted to the oldest cover-up there is—and the best," Dad said. "He just didn't remember struggling with the Sheriff. He didn't remember the cat either, or why he stopped to stare into the store window. A dizzy spell—and a total loss of memory."

Dad shook his head. "Amnesia that lasts for weeks or months is less easy to fake. But when it just takes in a period of an hour or so immediately preceding a shock it can be made almost ironclad—if you're careful and answer cautiously every question that's put to you. Poor Anderson! He was no match for the lad's mother either. She arrived in a fury, prepared to put up bail if necessary and determined to see that he was released immediately.

"She said it had happened twice before and the least that Anderson could have done was to see that he was treated with kindness and respect and guided safely home. A neurological specialist had assured her that her son's condition wasn't serious, and that he had simply been taking his graduate studies too seriously. In eight more months he'd be a Ph.D. and then if some ignoramus of a county sheriff stepped out of line and made a fool of himself—and an outrageously unfeeling fool at that—the whole academic world would be up in arms against him."

I was far more shaken than I wanted Dad to suspect and seized upon the first cover-up—it was almost as old as the one Bellamy had used—that came into my head.

"Why would the News-Chronicle publish a story like that, Dad?" I asked. "It's supposed to be a Reform Party newspaper. They backed Sheriff Anderson in the last election. Why should they hold him up to ridicule?"

Dad rose to the bait, as I'd known he would. A political, social, or economic challenge never fails to drive every other thought from his mind and he immediately started to dissect modern journalism in all of its ramifications, good, bad and indifferent.

"Bobby, despite all of your undoubted brilliance you sometimes appall me," he said. "How naive can you get? What do you suppose would happen to the circulation

99

of a newspaper—any newspaper, big city or medium-sized town—that adhered to a policy of absolute consistency in its presentation of the news? What you read on the editorial page is one thing, the news-section coverage quite another. In fact—"

"That isn't what the cynics say, exactly," I countered, before he could go on.

"What do the cynics say, exactly?" he demanded. "We may as well thrash this out right now."

"They say that all of the news is made to conform to the political coloration you find on the editorial page."

"I hope you realize how nonsensical that is," Dad said. (His expression couldn't have been more serious if he was at one of his Thursday night poker games, sending two blue chips spinning out into the middle of the table).

I could have dropped out of the game right then and there, for it was getting on toward nine, and Mom would hardly agree with Dad that I was a quitter if I got up and looked at the clock and told him we'd thrash it out some other time.

But my thoughts were in a ferment and I had a picture of Sheriff Anderson letting Bellamy out of his cell with a lot of things I'd like to know locked up in his mind.

Bellamy's address might not be in the News-Chronicle, but I could get it easily enough. All I needed was a little more time to set Dad's suspicions—if he had any—completely at rest.

What could I say, I wondered, that would make him think his talk with Anderson was already receding in my mind and of far less importance than the political hot potato of a newspaper's consistency, or lack of it, in the presentation of the news.

The answer came without much straining, and I turned it over in my mind and decided it was a good one.

"If news has real shock value," I said, "no newspaper is going to pass it up completely. But it's very easy to bring an item of that kind into harmony with a paper's political orientation. All you have to do is to put everything that reflects unfavorably on the party the paper is backing in quotes and bring in some feather-brained individuals to do the talking. You make them sound so silly you begin to feel a deep respect and admiration for the man they're talking about."

"Now you're *really* going far out!" Dad said. "How can you believe for a moment—"

Mom came out of the kitchen before he could complete whatever it was he'd started to say, and I breathed a sigh of relief.

"Why do you have to do this!" she said, looking up at the clock. "I'm getting terribly angry, Roger. I mean it. You're deliberately making him late for school—"

To my surprise Dad looked apologetic. I've never seen Mom look quite so angry and I guess he knew she had justice on her side.

"All right," he said, getting up and gathering up the two sections of the News-Chronicle which had fallen to the floor. "We were having a small argument and I didn't realize how late it was. Don't worry—he'll get there on time."

"I do worry and you know it," Mom said. "It's important for him to have a good attendance record. He's never missed a day or been late once this year."

"It won't matter twenty years from now," Dad said, sighing.

"What kind of talk is that?" Mom demanded. "How can you be so cynical in front of your own son? Suppose one of the bank's messengers disappeared with a million dollars in negotiable bonds. Would you tell the Board of Directors it won't matter twenty years from now?"

"Actually it wouldn't matter at any time," Dad said. "The bank is insured against such losses."

"Someone would lose," Mom said. "Someone would

101

have to suffer. Bonding companies have stockholders, don't they? Everything you do or fail to do sets in motion a train of consequences someone has to pay for in the end. If Bobby should be late for school just this one morning because of your inconsideration—"

"All right," Dad said. "You may consider me properly reprimanded."

9 CHARLES BELLAMY

I DIDN'T like what mother had told the Sheriff. Not that it mattered too much. No one would have believed any part of my story anyway, and I haven't a martyr complex. The Sheriff wasn't a bad sort, all things considered. But I'm claustrophobic about being locked up in a cell. Mother knows that and came to my rescue just in time.

It was a crazy idea anyway—the whole thing was crazy. When I was an undergraduate it was all right for me to be a door-to-door salesman from June to October. But what kind of occupation is that for a man who'll have his Ph. D. in nine months and is getting assistant professorship offers from a college that doesn't believe you always have to start at the bottom of the academic stepladder and work your way up by writing articles for obscure scholarly periodicals no one ever reads.

If the encyclopedia people hadn't offered me a special bonus because I'd done so well in the past and could talk housewives into buying almost anything I never would have considered it. Actually the payoff was two or three times what a summer teaching job would have brought me. But even so—

Everyone who has tried it knows that, soberly considered, door-to-door salesmanship isn't quite the discouraging, difficult to succeed in field that it's commonly thought to be. That's the one thing that can be said in its favor. Few people are so irate and unreasonable as to actually slam the door in your face, and it's seldom necessary to wedge your foot in the door until you've convinced them that you don't conform at all to the popular conception of how a salesman should talk and behave if he hopes to achieve success. If you know how to be outgoing without being in the least blustery or over-assertive your success is likely to verge, at times, on the miraculous.

It doesn't even do any harm to seem a little shy, if you're sufficiently charming and relaxed.

Encyclopedia salesmen have the additional advantage of being in a position to peddle from door to door the sum total of all human knowledge, handsomely packaged in leather and gold.

I'd passed the old Jonathan Oakham mansion many times as a youngster without dreaming that I might someday find myself opening the ornate, rustily creaking gate and crossing the front lawn with a briefcase in my hand.

Old Jonathan Oakham was a pretty formidable character and if he'd still been occupying the mansion the possibility that I might be able to interest him in a ten-volume encyclopedia wouldn't even have crossed my mind. It could almost be taken for granted that he had at least three sets, and a floor-ceiling shelf of other books that took care of everything the encyclopedias had left out.

But new tenants were occupying the mansion now, and the furniture they had just put in—I'd happened to be passing when the moving van was unloading—hadn't looked very Jonathan Oakham-like to me. No bookcases at all—let alone a floor-to-ceiling one. What could I lose by trying to talk them into starting with an encyclopedia and building a library around it across the years? A great many people start that way and gradually acquire an interest in literature, history, architecture and painting.

It's pleasant to feel that you've broadened the cultural horizons of people in the prime of life with many good years ahead of them and it seemed to me that it was at least worth a try.

The front door was adorned with both a brass knocker and a bell and I decided to try the bell first. The instant I pressed it it rang hollowly through the house. I waited and presently heard footsteps approaching the door and knew that I had done the right thing.

I was even more convinced of that when a chain rattled and a woman of perhaps thirty-five stood framed in the doorway with a slight look of annoyance in her eyes. The annoyance didn't mean a thing. Can it ever when a vision of total loveliness seems to come floating toward you on the wings of the morning and the down-streaming sunlight brings out all the highlights in a tumbled mass of hair, each individual strand of the sheerest spun-gold? It made the beautiful oval of her face seem framed in gold as well.

I can't honestly say she was the most beautiful woman I had ever seen. But she was certainly one of the three or four most beautiful.

"Well?" she said, with a slight harshness in her voice. Even that didn't spoil it. Nothing could.

For a moment I couldn't say anything, and to cover my confusion started fumbling in my briefcase for a circular which would explain exactly why I was there and the "wise purchase" feeling everyone had when they glanced through just the first volume of what was unquestionably the best encyclopedia buy of the century. But somehow my heart wasn't in it. All I really wanted to do was go right on staring at her.

She seemed to lose patience and was just starting to close the door when a man's voice, sharply raised, came from quite far inside the house, as if he hadn't heard the bell ring or was shouting to her not to take so long in answering it.

I couldn't catch the words themselves, but I'm quite sure that she did, for a look of sudden alarm came into her eyes and she lost no time in closing the door in my face.

She hadn't closed it quite fast enough, however and just before it slammed shut the man called out to her again and this time I heard him clearly.

"Where are you, woman? I'm stone deaf and my sight's going fast. We've delayed too long! They'll know what to do, but we've got to get to the cave before it's too late."

Most salesman, I'm quite sure, would have known better than to ring the bell again and then pound on the door when no answer was forthcoming. They would have simply swung about and left, with at least a few shreds of their dignity intact.

In the course of a single month a door-to-door salesman usually runs into more than one furious family quarrel and overhears words that are startling and make very little sense. But they would make sense if he had a background knowledge of what the quarrel was all about. He has the good sense, as a rule, to realize that, and doesn't let what he has overheard stand in the way of a swift, dignified departure. Only Charles Bellamy had to be different in that respect! Different in a great many other ways as well perhaps, for I've never been a philosophically complacent type, and find it hard to simply shrug off occurrences that are strange and mysterious, and make no attempt to get to the bottom of them.

It could have been no more than a family quarrel,

despite the wild words that had followed the unmistakably harsh: "Where are you, woman?" When a man has
a bitter grievance against his wife he can accuse her of
driving him both deaf and blind. But seldom in quite so
frantic a way, as if he feared the very thing he was accusing her of would come to pass. . . . And what
could he possibly have meant by: "They'll know what to
do. We've got to get to the cave before it's too late."

I kept pounding on the door for a full minute and
then gave it up, feeling somehow that the woman would
have opened the door again to explain, if not actually to
apologize, if she could possibly have done so. You don't
slam a door in a visitor's face without giving him some
explanation—not when he has overheard something that
would give the townsfolk a great deal to gossip about.
I was just a door-to-door salesman to her, and to give
a man whose right to be treated with courtesy should
be respected on that account alone the equivalent of a
slap in the face was a very foolish thing for a new resident to do.

Was the need to calm and reassure her husband so
urgent that it was keeping her occupied? Or was she
totally incapable of thinking of something to say to me
that would make his shouted words conform to a pattern of sanity that would be acceptable to a man who
would have little patience with evasiveness?

I'd turned and was crossing the front lawn with anger
and frustration making me tremble a little when I saw
the cat. It was a big, battle-scarred Tomcat, just about
the ugliest looking animal of its kind I'd ever seen. Its
green eyes glittered in the sunlight, and I had the feeling
it was watching every move I made.

I wasn't in the least disturbed by that—at first. A
savage-looking dog that watches you intently and growls
deep in its throat when you cross a lawn over which it
likes to think it holds undisputed sovereignty can never

106

be ignored with a shrug. But though cats can be almost as dangerous at times, their rage seldom erupts unless you back them into a corner or attempt to pick them up when they don't want to be stroked.

I didn't even become disturbed when I passed out into the street through the rusty iron gate and saw that the cat was following me. Ill-treated cats are always in search of a new master and will follow almost anyone who gives them a second glance. I had no particular reason to believe that particular cat had been ill-treated, beyond the fact that his ugliness might have made even a kindly-disposed master—or mistress—a little harsh with him at times. But there was certainly nothing unusual or disturbing about being trailed by a cat for a block or two. Once, in fact, a cat followed me all the way home and mother had warned me not to give it a platter of milk, for when you do that cats feel that they have been accepted and settle down as permanent guests.

All I really needed was to have the ugly-looking beast that was taking care to remain a cautious distance behind me turn into a guest in the house, and I forced myself to go right on walking without giving him the slightest encouragement to follow me. When I reached the end of the block and crossed over to the opposite side of the street I had the feeling he hadn't vanished, but I remained stubbornly determined not to look back to make sure. If I completely ignored him, I told myself, he'd probably go back to the Jonathan Oakham mansion and resign himself to being ill-treated again, if not by his mistress, by every small boy in the neighborhood with enough cruelty in his nature to enjoy chasing—and making life in general more difficult for—so huge and ugly-looking a cat.

Finally I did look back, just once, and saw that the animal was still following me. I was three blocks from

107

the Jonathan Oakham mansion now and walking so rapidly that the cat must have had to run to keep up with me. That struck me as peculiar. A cat so determined to accompany me home that he was behaving more like a stray puppy than a feline, stopping when I stopped and then racing after me as fast as his legs would carry him.

I began to walk even more rapidly, telling myself that being trailed along the street by a big cat in search of a new home was highly amusing and that letting it worry me made no sense at all. Surely I had more important things to worry about, including a thesis that would have to be finished by November at the latest.

I'd just reached the next corner when a wave of dizziness swept over me, forcing me to come to an abrupt halt. I seldom have dizzy spells and that such a bad one had overtaken me on the street without warning was certainly far more disturbing than just being trailed by a cat. Was it possible that Dr. Cowles had been mistaken when he'd thumped me over in June and assured me that I was in splendid physical shape?

The dizziness passed quickly enough. But it had given me so bad a moment that I completely forgot about the cat until I'd walked another full block.

I had left the curb and was crossing the street when I experienced something more alarming than a dizzy spell. I began to lose all control over my legs. They grew unsteady and I couldn't seem to continue on without losing my balance and tottering, first from left to right, and then forward in a staggering gait. But no feeling of dizziness accompanied that sudden, strange loss of control over my limbs. Even my arms were affected and when I tried to raise them to maintain my balance—there was nothing to hold on to, but I felt that holding them straight out might help—they fell limply back to my side.

For an instant I went tottering forward with so

108

violent a lurch that I was sure I'd find myself on the pavement before I could regain my balance.

But I didn't fall. At least my body didn't. I went tottering on, and the fear that I had lost all control over my movements no longer frightened me.

Something else did. It was a much more destructive kind of fright, for it made me doubt my sanity. My body continued on, but I remained apart from it, completely detached and following it as if from a distance. The distance increased as it gradually ceased to totter and approached the curb with only a slight swaying. I watched it ascend the curb and go shambling on down the street, leaving me a half block behind. I was just about where the cat had been and my movements were becoming clumsy and very slow and as I advanced over the pavement it seemed to me that my claws—*claws!* Oh, God, no!—were making a scraping sound.

The nightmare that followed didn't end until I found myself in a cell at the jail, with the Sheriff doing his best to calm me down and talk some sense into me. I'd calmed down quite a bit when he'd made it possible to get back inside my own body again, but he had no way of knowing that and he seemed to feel that I was still in a state of shock—which, of course, I was to some extent. But I managed to answer all of the questions he asked me and I remembered enough of what I'd once read about amnesia to keep him from accusing me of being a liar to my face. He wanted to, I was sure of that. In fact, I don't think he believed me at all when I told him I'd had a memory blackout. But when mother came she scared him a little, and I went along with what she told him, because I had no choice. It could jeopardize my entire academic career if the University found out about it, but that part didn't appear in the News-Chronicle, and just the fact that the University is in another state made mother decide to take the risk.

109

Perhaps I did have a kind of memory blackout. Even now I can't be sure that what seemed to happen after I left the Jonathan Oakham mansion actually took place. The human mind is the greatest of all mysteries and it can sometimes create illusions that are so solid and three-dimensional they seem to have been carved in granite. And what happened to me—or what I thought happened—wasn't anything like as solid as that, even though it seemed to take place in *more* than three dimensions.

I thought it wise not to tell the Sheriff anything. But I found it much more difficult to keep from telling Bobby Jackson everything when he came calling yesterday afternoon. He has a way of looking at you as if he could see deep into your mind and in the end I found myself trusting him completely.

He'd gotten my address from the Sheriff—Anderson and his dad have been close friends for twenty years—and mother surprised me by calling upstairs to announce his arrival a little after one. "You have a young visitor, Charles. He has something important he wants to talk to you about."

I went to the head of the stairs and looked down as he ascended. A "young visitor" could have meant a lad of eighteen or a much younger boy and I was curious as to how youthful he might be. He was very young indeed—not more than thirteen or fourteen. It was hard to imagine how a boy that young could have anything very important to discuss with me—unless he'd heard I had academic affiliations and could give him some advice about how to crash an Ivy League college when he finished high school. But that I doubted. At fourteen college still seems very remote to most youngsters—even though it's only three or four years away.

I recognized him before he was half-way up the stairs. Of course! Bobby Jackson, the Banker's son. From all

110

reports a brilliant youngster who might very well be a college graduate before he was nineteen.

It happens sometimes. But it wasn't in the cards in his case, as I found out a few minutes after I'd greeted him and put him at his ease and he was seated opposite me by the window in what I liked to call my study. He was in the eighth grade, which is just about average for a boy of fourteen, although some make it at twelve. That didn't surprise me too much, because a great many young geniuses don't tear through school at an above-average speed, and are glad that they didn't later on.

But his educational progress wasn't what he'd come to talk to me about, as I found out quickly enough.

He was interested in the Jonathan Oakham mansion too, and he had a great deal to tell me about it and the more he talked the more excited I became and I ended by telling him practically everything I knew.

I told him exactly why I'd gone there, and how I'd stood for a moment at a complete loss for words when Mrs. Martin had opened the door—he wasn't too young to understand the reason for that and wouldn't have been too old if he'd been in his ninety-third year—and how she'd slammed the door in my face, but not before I'd heard her husband calling out to her.

"Are you sure it was her husband?" Bobby Jackson asked.

"It was the voice of a middle-aged man," I said. "That's the only thing I can be sure of."

"Are you absolutely sure he called out: 'They'll know what to do! We've got to get to the cave before it's too late.'"

"Yes, those were his exact words," I assured him. "I don't think I'll ever be able to forget them."

"And right after that you rang the bell again and pounded on the door. That must have alarmed them. Enough probably to—"

111

He hesitated, and I had the strange feeling that he knew exactly what was passing through my mind. He seemed satisfied that he wasn't going to surprise or startle me too much and went on earnestly: "I think they knew that when you crossed the lawn to the gate you'd notice the cat crouching there watching you. And they took it for granted that you wouldn't be very surprised if it followed you out the gate and along the street for several blocks. Cats have a way of doing that sometimes when they encounter perfect strangers, and feel that a new home might be preferable to one they've grown to dislike. It would take a little time for the Martins to bring about—"

Again he hesitated, but I nodded for him to go on.

"Well . . . a *transference*," Bobby Jackson said.

"Man into cat. Is that what you mean?" I asked, feeling that he knew what I would say before the words left my lips.

"And cat into man," he replied, nodding.

"But why, Bobby?" I asked. "What could they hope to accomplish by it?"

"I'm not quite sure," he said. "Probably your eventual destruction. When it happened to me I felt that I was in terrible danger. I don't know just what would have happened if Mrs. Martin hadn't brought me out of it."

"Sheriff Morrison brought me out of it," I said. "When he kicked that cat—"

For a moment my throat seemed to tighten up, and I couldn't go on.

Bobby Jackson helped me. "I know," he said. "It wasn't just a cat he kicked and sent careening toward the curb. You felt no pain, however. I'm sure of that. The transference wasn't physical, couldn't have been."

"I felt no pain," I told him. "But it did save me."

"Probably because there are limitations to what the Martins can accomplish," he said. "You were a great

112

distance from the Jonathan Oakham mansion and so violent a shock—"

"Isn't it possible the spell may have just snapped by itself?" I asked. "What the Sheriff did may not have had anything to do with it."

"It's quite possible," Bobby Jackson said. "It isn't too important. The transference was shattered and that's all that really matters. It proves that destroying you wasn't as easy as the Martins had hoped it might be."

"You said the transference wasn't physical," I said, puzzled. "But Sheriff Anderson has scratches on his arm to prove that a cat in the body of a man attacked him."

"It was physical to that extent, obviously," Bobby Jackson said. "But not to the extent that you'd feel pain if you were injured while the transference was giving you a cat's sight and hearing and enabling to move about as if you had actually turned into cat."

"I could move the cat's legs?"

"Yes. And it could move your arms and legs and the rest of your body as well. But the transference, I'm convinced, was largely mental. That's not a very good term, but it's better and less confusing than 'psychic. The phenomenon is so strange, so alien to normal experience, that it's very hard to be certain as to just how completely the cat was transformed when it occupied your body or how completely you were transformed when you looked out on the world through the eyes of a cat. The cat's body felt pain when the sheriff kicked it, and it screeched. But your mind felt no pain at all. When it happened to me I felt for a moment that I was actually sharing, so some extent at least, the thoughts and emotions of a cat. Probably the transference is neither stable nor ever entirely complete. It must waver and change a great deal, from moment to moment."

"I only know that it was a ghastly experience," I said. "I would not care to have it happen again."

"I shall do my best to see that it doesn't," Bobby Jackson said.

I stared at him for a moment incredulously, hesitating to put what I thought into words for fear of causing him pain.

"I know," Bobby said, a slight smile of understanding hovering for an instant on his lips. "What can a boy my age possibly hope to accomplish? That's what you were thinking."

I looked at him and said nothing.

"It is only natural for you to think that," he went on, the smile vanishing. "But you've given me a key that may unlock a very dark and hidden door. When Mr. Martin—I've no doubt at all that it was his voice you heard—called out: 'We must get to the cave before it is too late,' I'm sure you must have known what cave he was referring to."

"Of course," I said. "Gower Cavern."

"It is not one cavern, but a series of interlocking caves covering almost a square mile," he said. "There is no other cavern like it in the vicinity of Lakeview. No other cave, in fact—even a small one. So that narrows it down considerably."

"You don't have to tell me that," I said. "I was born in Lakeview, and so was my grandfather."

"I thought so," he said. "But I wasn't sure. Tell me —have you ever been there?"

I shook my head. "Very few people have, apparently. I've often wondered why."

"And you were never curious enough to explore the cave yourself, even as a boy?"

"No . . . I never have," he said.

"Well, I've been there often," I said. "But not in the last few years."

And that's how our conversation ended, that was the whole of it.

114

I accompanied him downstairs to the front door and hardly knew what to say to him as he turned to leave. "Drop in any time, Bobby," seemed much too casual, in view of the gravity of what we'd been discussing.

He solved it for me by saying simply, "Goodbye, Mr. Bellamy. What you've told me is going to help. We'll keep in touch."

As soon as the front door closed behind him I went back upstairs and sat down again in the chair I'd just vacated. I had several very serious questions to ask myself.

Bobby Jackson had said something I couldn't put out of my mind. He'd mentioned it only once in the course of our conversation, and had seemed reluctant to dwell upon it. But we both knew that it was central to everything we'd been talking about. Even the terrifying implications of what had happened to me after I'd left the Jonathan Oakham mansion had only a kind of fragmentary importance in relation to the dark core of a mystery that went much deeper.

"I'm convinced," he'd said. "That the Martins aren't human at all."

I looked at him steadily for a moment, waiting for him to go on, feeling that he would if I said nothing in reply.

He didn't disappoint me. "I'm convinced they are just —*bodies*," he said. "Perhaps not even of flesh and blood but of that I am not sure. Bodies that have been given the power to think and feel in some wholly unnatural way."

I'd still kept silent, and just how he'd managed to steer the conversation at that point into other channels was a mystery in itself. It was so skillfully accomplished that it didn't even give me the feeling that it was deliberate on his part and that he didn't want me to question

115

him at length as to precisely what he'd meant by "unnatural."

But the strange mind-block which he'd somehow managed to impose was gone now, and I started thinking in a serious way about the role which artificial men and women, and the living dead and Frankenstein monsters have played in human thinking.

It's one of the great, elusive enigmas which have never been completely explored in depth, despite all that has been written about the unknown in the realm of imaginative fiction.

Just why are we so swayed and morbidly thrilled by the spectacle of a corpse walking, or some anatomical horror with clublike feet and a brain that is, paradoxically, both mindless and malignant? Why should we be both chilled and thrilled to such an extent that we deliberately prolong our exposure to a spectacle—on stage or screen—that should cause us to recoil in horror and blot what we have seen from our minds?

What happens to the defense-mechanism which we can summon to our aid when we want to forget the most unendurable of our waking world experiences outside of the theater or in the pages of a book—a man or woman trapped in a burning building with all hope of rescue cut off, a paralytic in a hospital ward breathing his last or a blind beggar, palsied with age, tottering along a street thronged with holiday merrymakers?

Is it because there exists, in the depths of our minds, an imprisoned something that knows what it means to be dead and cut off from all hope and is thus able to identify itself with the shambling monsters of nightmare and gibbering, ghoul-like creatures from beyond the grave?

Are we, in a sense, making laboratory experiments upon ourselves, picturing ourselves in a Boris Karlov role lying anaesthetized upon a table, and watching that

116

buried part of ourselves waking slowly and horribly to life as the lightning flashes all around us?

Why, when we have read Henry James' *TURN OF THE SCREW* do we return to it again and again, as if we could see that buried something hideously mirrored in the web of darkness that is slowly and relentlessly enmeshing the two terrified children?

Might it not be that stories of vampires and were-wolves evoke much the same kind of hypnotic fascination—snake-eyed in its malignancy—because the man-into-beast transformation sets off an almost identical trigger-mechanism deep in our minds?

Isn't the reanimation of the dead the most dreadful and at the same time the most compulsively irresistible theme in the whole of literature—even though the great masters of the genre are so few that it does not play a major role in human creativity—solely because to imagine a tenement of once living flesh restored to life in an unnatural way brings us face to face with the unknown in a confrontation that is inescapably stark and just as inescapably unyielding?

We are brought to bay by that dreadfulness, like some laboratory animal cruelly trapped in a blind maze, goaded beyond endurance by something that it cannot hope to understand but knows that it must submit to.

The reanimation of the dead can take subtle and disguised forms, and sometimes it need not even be the dead who are reanimated to shamble, monsterlike, away from the laboratory table.

Surely to construct a fleshly tenement from inanimate matter—no matter how outwardly radiant the man or woman shape may be—and breathe into it the spark of life is to strip the human mind of all of its defenses.

With Bobby sitting opposite me, my own defenses had seemed momentarily in abeyance. There was something extraordinary about him, a maturity and a perceptive-

117

ness impossible to reconcile with his chronological age. Outwardly he was a tousle-haired youngster, with a bridge of freckles across his nose. Inwardly—

How could I have allowed him to guide my thoughts as he had, sometimes almost with an air of impatience, as if by pursuing a train of thought he had himself suggested I was preventing him from evaluating the information I had given him, and fitting it into a pattern that would be useful to him?

Useful to him in accomplishing what? I remembered other things he'd said—things that now, in retrospect—seemed strange beyond belief.

"A new kind of man," he'd said, "may be evolving from what we have allowed ourselves to think of as a mould into which all of humanity has been cast. How can we be sure that the mould can not be broken? The existence of such a superbeing in our midst might be mankind's sole protection against cold, inscrutable intelligences from other worlds."

"'And you think mankind is in need of such protection now?" I'd asked.

"I'm sure of it," he said. "What happened to you when you left the Jonathan Oakham mansion was not an isolated occurrence. I had a similar experience and there is little doubt in my mind that it has happened to others. So far rarely, perhaps, and those who know or suspect the truth may have been silenced."

"Killed?" I asked.

"Or taken captive. I believe they are proceeding cautiously, step by step. Can everyone in Lakeview be made to believe that the Martins are as human as you or I, respected members of a community that does not mistrust newcomers who do not appear to have been living without roots or social responsibility elsewhere? They will have to wait and see. In the early stages of such an experiment many things could go wrong, so that

118

anyone stumbling on the truth prematurely would have to be silenced."

"And eventually?"

"If the experiment succeeds there will be many Martins, in every village and city on Earth. They will have been given their instructions and they will carry them out and—Earth will have been conquered."

Go back to Bobby's arrival, I told myself. When he first sat down opposite you and began to talk you certainly did not think of him as anything but a bright fourteen-year-old. Even when he left you did not feel, as you do now, that if there *is* a superbeing in our midst there might be no need to search for him any further than—

The glow appeared so suddenly on the opposite wall that for a moment I thought the wind had blown the shade aside, causing the room to be flooded with an almost blinding burst of sunlight. But sunlight cannot cause the solid walls of a room to dissolve and a dark shadow to emerge from the glow with a shining, knob-studded tube in its hand.

Straight toward me out of the glow the shadow walked, assuming as it advanced a human shape and then, more slowly, the face of a woman with burning eyes who kept the tube trained on me as the glow spread over the floor and ceiling and words formed in my brain.

"This is difficult for them. The binding energies of matter resist such dangerous tampering and the thermonuclear displacement may be of short duration. My body and the wall through which I have just passed have been converted by this tube into radiant energy. But the disintegration of your body will not be painful. You will not even be aware that it is taking place, and when you are restored to consciousness its atomic structure will have been restored also. But you must not move or I shall be forced to kill you."

119

Mrs. Martin stood very still, raising the shining tube until it was pointed directly at my head.

10 JOHN DYSON

I'D BEEN pacing the floor all morning, going to the window and back, and telling myself that at any moment I might see Laura crossing the street to my apartment, almost breathless from hurrying to put an end to my torment, and assure me that her disappearance had meant absolutely nothing and that there had been no need for me to get in touch with the Sheriff.

I had no regrets on that score. If her failure to reappear at the library after her departure for lunch the previous morning had caused so little alarm the young lady who took over her duties from eleven to twelve hadn't even taken the trouble to do any inquiring at all until late in the afternoon there were others who felt differently about it. The Sheriff was one of them. He knew Laura quite well and was quick to tell me when I phoned that she would feel the same way about neglecting her library duties as I would about walking out of the classroom on a bright September day with a fishing rod in my hand and leaving Bobby Jackson in charge.

He didn't mention Bobby, of course. But when you're almost beside yourself with worry and strain dire absurdities have a way of flashing across your mind and if you're wise you'll do your best to hammer them into a kind of shield, to protect you against possibilities even direr and the opposite of absurd.

Had Laura simply packed up and left town, without telling anyone where she had gone? *That*, at least, was absurd. She would have certainly told me. . . . It wasn't in Laura's nature to take what had happened between us so lightly that she could inflict so cruel a wound.

That she could have been struck by a car and taken to the Lakeview Hospital had to be ruled out as totally inconceivable, if only because she wasn't at the hospital and there had been no motor accident in Lakeview yesterday.

But what if—The thought was so frightening that for a moment I failed to realize how difficult it would be for some motorist who was hit-and-run vicious to stop, get out of the car, pick his victim up, and instead of running drive off with her, without leaving behind him a single witness to his crime.

No—there almost had to be some other explanation of why and how she had vanished. That it had happened between eleven o'clock and the noon hour, when a great many people were on the streets, made it seem even more inexplicable. Not more than four crimes of dark violence —the kind of violence I refused to even let myself think about—had occurred in Lakeview during the past ten years and all of them had taken place after dark.

If it hadn't been Saturday I would have had classroom problems to keep me occupied until some news came in, and would not have been compelled to pace back and forth at home in futile desperation. I wasn't helping Laura in any way, wherever she was—Oh, God, *wherever* she was—and I certainly wasn't helping myself.

I suddenly found myself thinking about Bobby Jackson again. Why did my thoughts always so persistently return to him when the sky became overcast in a peculiarly somber and threatening way? The day had started off overcast and now storm clouds were slowly gathering far to the east. A great mass of storm clouds that seemed to get darker as I stared at them.

I remembered the freak lightning bolt that had come zigzagging into the classroom and split up in so terrifying a way that I could only stare at Bobby in appalled silence as the fireball hung suspended in the air directly over his head.

What was it Bobby had started to tell me just before the lightning had been preceded by a roll of thunder that had almost deafened me? "I don't think everything would stop."

Well . . . everything had stopped for a moment, even the beating of my heart. Could everything have stopped for Laura in much the same way? And could the fireball that had hovered over Bobby's head without striking him down—

I was just turning from the window, wondering if another cigarette would help—it is strange how just the lighting of a cigarette can sometimes keep you from taking a fateful last step into darkness that you will never cease to regret—when the telephone rang.

It rang three times as I crossed to the table on which it stood and so great was my fear that I might not get to it before the ringing stopped that I almost didn't.

In uncradling the receiver I almost upset the phone and the table as well, and my hands were still shaking when I heard Bobby's voice ask over the wire: "Is that you, Mr. Dyson?"

Why did it have to be Bobby? Why couldn't it have been the Sheriff, telling me that Laura had been found, and wanted to speak to me herself, because she was determined to tell me, right in the Sheriff's presence, not only that she was safe and unharmed, but that she loved me very much? If only she could have said that and I could have said in reply: "You'll never know how much

122

I love you," all of the storm clouds far to the east would have vanished—for me at least.

But it was only Bobby speaking to me. What could he possibly have to tell me that would cause the storm clouds to lift?

"My. Dyson, are you listening? Can you hear me?" came urgently over the line, as if the click he'd heard when I'd lifted the receiver had convinced him that my silence was a little strange.

"Yes . . . I'm listening, Bobby," I said. "Just a minute while I untangle the wire. I didn't mean to take so long answering. But I've been under a severe strain."

"Is it because Miss Hartley—"

"I'm afraid it is," I said, cutting him short. "No word so far. I was hoping I'd hear from the Sheriff sometime this morning."

"He doesn't know where she is, Mr. Dyson," Bobby said. "But I do."

I was more than just startled. It sounded almost like something a kidnapper might say if he were bargaining about ransom terms with a stricken parent. Not that I suspected Bobby of being a kidnapper. But I'm a little ashamed of some of the thoughts I entertained for a minute or two.

How could he possibly know where Laura was unless he had some direct knowledge of the circumstances surrounding her disappearance? And if he possessed such knowledge why had he kept it a secret from the Sheriff? Surely he must have realized he was placing himself under a dark cloud of suspicion by refusing to take Anderson into his confidence and confiding only in me.

But if he actually did know the last thing I wanted to do was to antagonize him and make him think that I would go straight to the Sheriff with whatever he'd decided to tell me—perhaps solely because he wasn't blind and knew exactly how much Laura meant to me.

123

I'd let another long silence intervene, but this time I was sure it hadn't seemed strange to him, for he must have known how profoundly his words would shock me.

"Bobby?" I said.

"Yes, Mr. Dyson?"

"I'd find it hard to forgive you if I thought you weren't absolutely sure about what you've just said. I'd like to believe that you are."

"I know where she is, Mr. Dyson—and I'm going to try to set her free."

To set her free! For a moment I stood very still, gripping the receiver so tightly my fingers began to throb. "You mean someone is keeping her a prisoner? Just one man—or several men? You must know that too. *Tell me what happened, Bobby.* No matter how bad it is, Anderson will know what to do. He's dealt with kidnappers before."

"She wasn't kidnapped, Mr. Dyson. I mean—when people talk of kidnapping they're thinking of something quite different."

"If she's being held prisoner somewhere against her will it amounts to the same thing. What are you trying to do, Bobby? Torment me beyond endurance? Evasiveness doesn't make sense when there's no reason for you to keep any part of it from me."

"I won't, Mr. Dyson—if you'll meet me at Gower's Cave in half an hour. If you bring the Sheriff with you I won't be able to free her."

"I see. You strike a hard bargain, Bobby."

"It's a necessary bargain, Mr. Dyson."

"All right, Bobby," I said. "I'll be there."

"Alone, Mr. Dyson?"

"You give me no choice," I said.

That wasn't true, of course, and when I re-cradled the receiver I had every intention of waiting a moment and then getting the Sheriff on the phone.

I don't know what made me decide not too. I wasn't

124

sure it could even be called a decision. I only knew
that every time my hand went toward the phone something seemed to prevent me from uncradling the receiver
again. A kind of paralysis seemed to arrest my hand six
inches from the phone, but it wasn't so much a physical
paralysis as a complete failure of will.

11 BOBBY JACKSON

I COULD remember every trip I'd ever made to Gower
Cavern. When I was seven I used to go there three or
four times a month, whenever I had an urge to go poking
around with a flashlight in a mysterious, underground
world where everything seemed bigger than it was. Bigger
and more shadowy. The silence scared me, and so did
the shadows. But it gave me a thrill to think of myself
as a bold explorer, venturing deep into the earth in search
of hidden treasures.

Once or twice I'd let myself become kid-silly all the
way, even picturing myself as a coal miner with a lamp
strapped to my forehead and a pick on my shoulder. Out
in the sunlight again I'd tell myself it was a good thing
no one knew how childish I could be in my thoughts at
times, and I guess it was the way I felt about the need
of keeping all that to myself which made those early
visits to the cave stick in my memory.

When you can stand by a riverbank and thrill to the
fall of the rain and see through the turbulent water a
rainbow trout heading upstream and feel that you are

125

very close to the breathing, pulsing core of nature herself
. . . how can you be no different from Willie Simpson
with his toy fire engine or Jackie McClary with his red and
yellow scooter in another part of your mind?

Ask me no riddles and I'll tell you no lies. There are
some things I'm sure that not even Kant could have ex-
plained if he'd brought all of his cold logic to bear upon
them, and it's quite possible that at seven or eight the
author of *The Critique of Pure Reason* was a tow-headed
little mischief-maker who was always getting into fistfights
while his thoughts ranged through eternity and mocked
the absurdity of bruised knuckles and mud-spattered
pants.

A sudden gust of wind from outside the cave whirled
dust in my eyes, and the stinging sensation brought me
sharply back to a reality so grim and fraught with danger
that all of the far off childhood memories I'd let myself
dwell on for a moment seemed to go spiraling away into
the darkness through which I was moving, with Mr. Dyson at my side. It was curious how memories which
went back only seven years could seem so far-off at
times that the years in between might just as well have
numbered fifty or a hundred.

I knew that if I turned to Mr. Dyson abruptly now
and asked him: "Who is Laura Hartley" he'd have stared
at me with a look of bewildered incomprehension in his
eyes. I had wanted it to be that way—both for his
sake and mine—and it had taken me only a moment to
impose the memory block.

He'd been so wrought up and had questioned me so
wildly that it had begun to interfere with the absolute
calmness I was trying desperately to maintain. I had no
intention of removing the memory block until I was sure
it would be completely safe to do so. It could do him no
possible harm to believe—and I had implanted the thought
with care—that I had asked him to join me because

I was tremendously excited about a strange-looking geological formation in the depths of the cave I'd stumbled on quite by accident and could hardly wait to discuss with him, after he'd looked at it and seen for himself just how extraordinary it was.

I'd also made him believe that it fitted right in with the flying saucer talk we'd had in the classroom earlier in the week, because that would keep him alert and on guard.

I might or might not need his help. But if I did his inability to recall what I'd said to him on the phone would be of no importance. If I'd made a mistake in asking him to join me I would know soon enough. But I didn't think I had. To confront a very great danger absolutely alone is always a mistake—unless no help of any kind is available. Even if the outcome proves disastrous that does not mean that the decision itself was wrong. It only means that circumstances over which you have no control have taken a turn which could not possibly have been anticipated.

I knew that the main struggle would have to be waged alone, and that if my resolution wavered, even for an instant, I could not hope to save myself. But I knew that what I expected to encounter in a very large cavern close to the end of the interlocking series of caves might be too complex and many-taloned to overcome without assistance. When you tap on a dark, securely-guarded door and it opens silently on an even more terrible kind of darkness it is well to have someone standing by you have absolute confidence in and whose courage, at least, will remain steadfast.

It would not be long, I knew, before we would be unable to keep from stumbling about in total darkness without clicking on our flashlights. I had brought two flashlights with me and he was firmly clasping the one I had handed him. But there was still enough light from the entrance

127

to see by, and the only impediments under foot were scattered pebbles, and a few flat, slablike stones almost level with the soil.

During the eight or ten minutes which had passed since I'd made it impossible for him to remember Laura Hartley by implanting in his mind another reason for our visit to the cave, Mr. Dyson hadn't said a word.

Just the constantly widening width of the cave and the way the shadows danced and flickered on the walls as we advanced seemed to fascinate him, and make him forget, for a moment, not only the agitation and anxiety which I'd been forced to blot from his mind, but the tremendous discovery I'd convinced him I'd made. He seemed in no hurry to get to the non-existent rock structure which, if it had not been a deliberately imposed deception, would have made Unidentified Flying Objects a lively bone of contention between us again, with all of the evidence strongly supporting my side of the argument.

But Mr. Dyson was like that. It would not have been true to say he had a one-track mind. But sometimes, when his thoughts are traveling on just one track at breakneck speed he can't seem to switch to another track fast enough to avoid being derailed. He ignores the signal tower, the red lights and the frantically waving switchman and goes plunging on at his own peril. Sometimes that peril can be very great. But who was I to pick flaws in the armor of so unusual a man? He was stoutly encased in that armor most of the time, and could probably have survived a fall over a hundred foot cliff if he resolutely set his mind to it on the way down. I've often thought that if someone told him Lakeview was about to go up in smoke and flame and he had a composition on his desk that interested him he'd go right on talking about it until the walls of the classroom collapsed.

He was looking up at the roof of the cave now, as if the dangling outcroppings reminded him of stalactites and it had occurred to him that there might be bats up there as well. I knew that he would find no stalactites and that we would be unlikely to encounter any bats.

But Gower Cavern didn't have to be infested with bats to give an intruder the feeling that he was being spied upon by hobbling or flying shapes of darkness with sharp talons. There were grotesque shadows everywhere and the rock structure itself was pitted and glazed and had a melted-down look.

It resembled nothing so much as the interior of a hollowed out, mile-long meteor that had crashed down in the valley when the Earth was young and was sinking deeper into the ground with every passing millennium. Perhaps someday it would disappear.

I was suddenly aware that Mr. Dyson had come to an abrupt halt and was tugging at my arm. "We'd better not go any further until we've some stronger light to see by," he said. "There's a turn in the wall right up ahead and when we're on the other side of it we'll be in total darkness."

"All right, turn on your flashlight," I said. "There's no reason for us to risk tripping over stones the way we've been doing."

"Isn't there?" he asked, and I was startled by the concern in his voice. "I've a feeling there's something you've been keeping from me. I don't know a damn thing about geology, and even though we had that talk about flying saucers I can't see why you should have phoned me and been so insistent that I meet you here immediately. It could have waited until tomorrow. Sunday is the best day for exploring a cave like this, when you've put in a hard week at school. It takes a while for the cobwebs to thin out and this is a particularly overcast day anyway. Storm clouds have been massing all morning. I should imagine a sunny day would be more to your liking, after what happened in the classroom Tuesday."

129

So he'd remembered my phone call, even though I'd succeeded in making him forget that it had been about Laura Hartley!

"Sometimes it's hard to wait when you're all keyed up about something tremendous, Mr. Dyson," I said. "Besides, the weather report says it's going to rain all day tomorrow."

"You took the trouble to check on that, Bobby? Well, if it's that important to you I suppose I ought to go along without complaining. But I still have a strange feeling that you're concealing something from me. Are you?"

"Of course not, Mr. Dyson," I said. "Why should I be?"

"Maybe just to win an argument, Bobby. Even a startling looking rock formation can be—well, rearranged a little. A stone removed here and there and placed in a different position—"

Oh, what a tangled web we weave when first we practice to deceive. Was that just a silly platitude, I wondered, or did the poet who'd thought that one out really have something in the imperishable wisdom line? He was lying in his grave way back in the eighteenth century and there was no way I could travel back through Time and ask him.

Besides, the exploring I had to do was right up ahead, in the depth of a cave where that kind of wisdom or lack of it shriveled to insignificance. When you practice to deceive a cold and alien intelligence with a plan for Earth conquest with no margin for error in it that you can narrow without moving out over an abyss that can send you plunging to your death the web you weave becomes more than just tangled.

Mr. Dyson seemed almost instantly to regret having accused me of removing stones here and there from a rock formation that he had constructed from a televised image that I'd implanted in his mind solely to spare him pain—

130

though of course he had no way of knowing that—for he gave me a pat on the shoulder and we continued on in silence.

He'd switched on his flashlight and it illumed the ground ahead of us with so wide a swath of radiance that there was no need for me to use mine.

We reached the turn in the cave wall without stopping again. We encircled a large boulder and were just approaching another turn when Mr. and Mrs. Martin stepped out from the shadows on opposite sides of the wall.

Mr. Martin had a long, shining tube in his hand and it gave off so bright a glow that it completely outshone the light from Mr. Dyson's flash. Mrs. Martin just stood very still, empty-handed, and stared at me as if she hoped I wouldn't be alive to come any nearer before her husband leapt across the cavern to her side.

Mr. Martin must have had much the same thought and known exactly what she wanted him to do, for he raised the tube quickly and the beam started moving toward me.

It was a great mistake and the last one he ever made. I stood very still, feeling for an instant as if I had been turned into a pillar of flame. But it was just the heat which the beam gave off before Mr. Martin leapt back against the wall and let the tube drop to the ground. If the beam had traveled on and reached me I wouldn't have been able to stop him from training it on Mr. Dyson as well, because I would no longer have been there.

Making Mr. Martin bend double and clutch at his chest and open and close his mouth spasmodically, like a fish out of water struggling to breathe wasn't as difficult as I'd feared it might be. Slowly, relentlessly, I brought about his destruction by forcing him to turn all of the unnatural life in his writhing, convulsively trembling body upon himself. His mind, I knew, could be manipulated

131

and turned into a weapon that would rip that life to shreds if the right commands were issued, and the mental force that was brought to bear did not waver for an instant. I knew what those commands were and I had absolute confidence in my ability to make them prevail.

Remembering what he had done because he wasn't human, I experienced not the slightest stirring of guilt.

It was more difficult for me to bring about the destruction of Mrs. Martin. It left me so shaken that for a full minute after she'd stopped moving I couldn't stop thinking about how she might have looked if I'd come upon her unexpectedly in the autumn woods and she'd turned to gaze at me with the sunlight in her hair and there had been no need for her to fear me—and I had no reason to suspect that her great beauty had been designed to mask an inhuman mechanism with a coldly merciless artificial brain.

What I had been forced to do might have been even more unendurable if I'd had more time to dwell on how she looked now—crumpled and lifeless and strangely shrunken, with sightlessly staring eyes. But there were four others and they came around the turn in the cave wall just as I was bending to examine the shining tube which had fallen from Mr. Martin's hand.

Mr. Dyson cried out warningly when he saw them and leapt back, and that gave me the few seconds I needed to recover from the shock which I received when I recognized them and make sure that they would never walk again.

Fred Halstrom, the garage mechanic, was the first to go reeling backwards against the cave wall. Samuel Thompson, the athletic instructor at Lakeview High was a sturdily built man in the prime of life, but that didn't prevent him from collapsing just as rapidly as Mr. Martin had done. Clifford Andrews had been a bookworm most of his life and the stooped over position which he instantly assumed seemed almost natural to him. But there

132

was nothing natural about the way he tottered and went spinning about, clutching at his chest until he fell, with a convulsive shudder, to the ground. Theodore Murch, whom I'd always thought of as a Lakeview version of the man in the gray flannel suit, took almost two minutes to collapse, reeling backwards against the cave wall as Fred Halstrom had done and then sinking jerkily to his knees.

A wave of dizziness swept over me then and for an instant I felt I might be in danger of blacking out. The effort had drained me of almost all my physical strength, although I hadn't taken a single step forward or so much as raised my arm.

Mr. Dyson must have seen me sway, for he lost no time in gripping me by the shoulders and supporting me until the dizziness passed.

He was breathing harshly and I knew that what I'd been forced to do had come as a great shock to him. He hadn't even known that the Martins weren't human. And if I'd tried to explain about the others he would have been even more appalled and incredulous and would almost certainly have refused to believe me.

What would he have thought, I found myself wondering, if I'd said: "Those four men lying there aren't really Mr. Thompson, Mr. Andrews, Mr. Murch, and Mr. Halstrom at all. They were made to resemble—to be exact replicas, in fact—of Thompson, Andrews, Murch, and Halstrom, because their human counterparts happen to be highly individual Lakeview characters. They stand out without being conspicuously eccentric, and no one would be at all surprised to have one of them as a next-door neighbor.

"When once you've grasped the importance of that the next step shouldn't be difficult. In every city and village on Earth there are a great many Andrews, Thompsons, Halstrom and Murches—or their equivalents in terms of next-door neighborliness. So if experiments are to be made it would make sense to start with character types that are likeable, ingratiating and easily recognizable.

"You see, Mr. Dyson, paradoxical as it may seem, it's the completely colorless, run-of-the-mill types who are most likely to come under suspicion when they do or say anything that's even slightly unusual. To avoid all suspicion it is necessary to both conform and not conform to accepted patterns of community behavior in a highly individualistic way. Mr. Martin was highly individualistic in his conformity, and that is why they thought he would be the character type most likely to succeed. He was the first, but next month or next year an Andrews, Thompson, Halstrom or Murch who isn't human at all would have probably replaced their human counterparts in Lakeview.

"Who would know, who would suspect that the athletic instructor at Lakeview High School, or the Lakeview equivalent of the man in the gray flannel suit, or the quiet, amiable little man with a liking for books were inhuman mechanisms with artificial brains and ingeniously constructed bodies?"

I suddenly realized I was making a great mistake. Mr. Dyson would have to be told everything now. He had received so terrible a shock that if I attempted to silence the questions he would be certain to ask any memory block I might impose would have to be almost the equivalent of a prefrontal lobotomy. And that would strip away too much of his personality. It was something I had no right to do.

It would have to be told, and whether he believed me or not would be for him to decide.

I knew I would have to keep my explanation brief. We were in the deadliest kind of danger and would have to press on swiftly and reach the great central cavern close to the end of the long series of caves before it was too late. The cavern was open to the sky and there would

134

be a great deal of light there, but not the kind of light that Mr. Dyson now so desperately needed.

With the bodies of five men and one woman who hadn't been human at all lying sprawled out in grotesquely distorted attitudes close to the turn in the cave wall passing around that turn and continuing on was not going to be easy for him. He would have to be told, and quickly.

I watched his face as I talked. I'd switched on my own flashlight and asked him to click his off, for his hand had been shaking violently and I wanted to keep the light steadily trained on the turn in the cave wall. There was enough light to enable me to see his features clearly.

At first there was a look of stark incredulity in his eyes, but gradually as I continued to talk I could see that he was beginning to believe me.

I don't know whether or not I succeeded in convincing him completely. It was hard to tell, just by observing how his expression changed, how much of what I said he was able to accept as something he could go right on living with.

When I'd finished he stood very still for a moment, staring down at the sprawled out bodies. In falling Mrs. Martin had forgotten that beauty and a graceful posture in a woman are inseparably linked, and now, somehow, she no longer looked beautiful or even entirely human. Her hair had fallen down over her face and her features were hidden. But there was something lumpish about the once graceful form, as if the mechanism had begun to unwind before she'd stopped moving and brought about the kind of destructive changes that are illusion-shattering.

When Mr. Dyson finally raised his eyes and looked at me I no longer had any doubt that he believed that he could still keep a tight grip on his sanity and accept most of what I'd told him. I could see as well, that as far as that acceptance went it was close to absolute. I would

135

have been surprised if it had been otherwise, for what he had seen with his own eyes supported almost everything I'd said and made it impossible for him to doubt that the six sprawled out bodies had been the opposite of human.

I removed the memory block then, completely.

When I saw the look of torment that came into his eyes I feared for an instant that I had made a mistake.

"You know where Laura is," he said. "But does that mean that you can save her?"

"Nothing is sure until it is accomplished," I told him. "But their minds are somnolent now. I do not think they know that we are here—or will have any way of knowing until they awaken. They are not infallible and although the Martins were keeping me under close observation there is a great deal that they haven't even begun to suspect about Bobby Jackson. They were depending on the Martins to guard the cave and warn them."

"There is a great deal that *I* do not know about Bobby Jackson," he said, and he spoke the words in so earnest a way, with such desperate appeal in his voice, that it was hard for me to pretend that I hadn't heard him. But I was already turning and I thought it best to continue on through the darkness, quite sure now that he would not fail to accompany me.

12 LAURA HARTLEY

I AWOKE and slept in fitful stages, never doubting that they were going to kill me. During lucid moments I saw only a blank gray wall, nine or ten feet from where I sat with my hands lashed together behind me, and moving up and down and across the wall, never wholly absent, a meaningless jumble of shifting lights and shadows.

How long, I wondered. Will it come when I am sleep, and so overcome with exhaustion that I will not be able to stir and cry out and plead with my executioners, even if I should awaken when they stand above me with their terrible weapons of destruction trained on me?

What will they be like, those weapons? What will *they* be like. Huge and formless, blending with the shadows, faceless but not without sight, and seeing me as a small, terrified creature so pitiful that they might be stirred to compassion—how many men would deliberately stamp on a toiling, heroically struggling ant?—if my destruction had not been made mandatory by what I had seen?

By what I had seen—yes. I knew that now. A face taken apart and remoulded to suit the purpose which they had implanted in a creature very different from the woman they were going to kill, because *he* was the opposite of unimportant to them.

How talkative the Martins were, when you really got to know them, Mr. Martin especially. He'd talked to me even when he'd had to accomplish a task that couldn't have been easy for him. Turning the wall of the restaurant into radiant energy and getting me through it with the aid of a shining tube that could have destroyed us both if he'd made the slightest miscalculation must have been most difficult.

But that hadn't prevented him from confessing what I had of course known the instant I'd seen him taking his face apart by the reading room window. He wasn't human at all—and neither was Mrs. Martin.

He'd warned me then that he would have to kill me, and when the words had formed in my mind I should have been forewarned and known how useless it was to

137

struggle when he came up behind me, and gripped me firmly by the shoulders in the restaurant.

The warning hadn't been quite accurate and he'd apologized for that too. What he'd really meant was that *they* would have to kill me. But they wanted to observe me closely for a short while first—to see just how demoralized I'd become and whether I'd still be capable of hating and defying them. I was to be a kind of living barometer which would enable them to gauge just how much resistance the human race would be likely to put up when there were Martins in every city and village on earth. I was one of the first to discover the truth about the Lakeview Martins and that made me of some importance to them. But for a short while only—a very short while. There was a young man they would have to kill too, and they were keeping him under observation in another gray-walled room, where the shadows moved up and down and across the wall and were never wholly absent and the Martins kept dropping in to talk to him just as they kept dropping in to talk to me. He was a door-to-door salesman, and he'd made the mistake of calling on the Martins at a very bad time—just when Mr. Martin was beginning to—well, run down. It happened every so often. His eyeballs would begin to throb and that was a warning sign. It meant that if he didn't get back to Gower Cavern very quickly he'd go both deaf and blind.

It would be all very amusing, in a way—a kind of bizarre comedy verging on the farcical—if it didn't happen to be true. And there's nothing farcical about the truth when you're sitting in a gray-walled room—or compartment, I suppose it should be called—and wonder why you don't start screaming inwardly more often.

No—it isn't amusing at all.

There were times when I could shut my eyes very tightly and dwell on another truth that could be almost comforting if you didn't shrink away from it the way so

138

many people do. Why should I be so afraid to die, when it happened to practically everyone? Can anything that universal ever be quite as bad as it's pictured? Would nature—despite all the cruelty you'll find in nature—be capable of staging an act of unreason on so colossal a scale? That death could be quite the way it's commonly pictured, I mean. There must be something about death, some hidden secret, we haven't discovered yet. And when we know that secret death may not be terrible at all.

The only trouble was—whenever I shut my eyes very tightly I began to grow drowsy from sheer exhaustion and there was nothing comforting about the dreams that came in a sleep that was interrupted by periods of wakefulness that were just as bad in another way and kept me tossing feverishly from side to side.

I didn't pay much attention to the glow when it appeared very dimly on the wall at first, because the shadows were always in motion and the lights had a way of shifting about also and seeming to grow brighter at intervals. For two or three minutes I completely ignored it —or tried to. I was almost sure that the shifting lights and shadows had been projected on the wall by mechanical means and were as much a part of the observation experiment and what was being done to my mind as the frequent visits of the Martins.

But the new light was the steadier and more stationary and it seemed to widen as it grew continuously brighter and after a moment I no longer had any doubt that a part of the wall was ceasing to be a solid, three-dimensional barrier to the figure that was coming through the wall with the light blazing all about him.

It could only be Mr. Martin, I told myself wildly, remembering what had happened in the restaurant. He had never entered the compartment that way before and if he was doing so now it could only mean—

The thought struck terror to my heart, and for an instant I could only stare at the intruder in the midst of the glow as if he were not coming through the wall alone but was accompanied by a towering figure with hollow eye-sockets and a gleaming scythe in its clasp.

It was surely the way that Death would come in such a place at such a moment, skeleton-thin and towering and following closely in the wake of a cruel and merciless destroyer who looked like a man, but wasn't even human.

Then, all at once, the scream that had almost been wrenched from my lips and that I would have been powerless to stop, that would have gone on and on until it became wholly animal-like and my breathing was stilled forever was shattered with the shattering of the illusion. I could feel it dying in my throat, that terrible, strangled shriek, dying in a million fragments as what I thought I'd seen became what it actually was, a night-dark phantom of the mind with no real existence at all, and the small form of Bobby Jackson emerged from the glowing wall with no towering, scythe-swinging figure at his back and with nothing whatever in his hand—not even a shining tube.

He spoke to me the instant he was at my side, and bending over to set me free. "Even a solid wall can be made permeable by the power of thought alone, if you try hard enough, Miss Hartley. That may seem unbelievable to you, but it is true. You could not do it, or Mr. Dyson. But I can, and I am not alone on Earth as I once feared. A new kind of man is coming into existence and I am one of the forerunners and I am not alone. There are hundreds . . . thousands . . . of others and more will be born in the generations ahead. Mutant genes—"

It was almost as if he were speaking to himself and not to me at all, and I had the feeling for a moment that his triumph had been so tremendous and complete that he was still a little stunned by it and needed the reassur-

140

ance that only his own voice could give him to accept it as completely real.

"We haven't much time," he went on quickly. "You must do exactly as I say, and not hesitate or draw back or doubt my ability to keep them from destroying you. Mr. Dyson is waiting for you in the cavern and you must join him and leave the cavern as quickly as you can. I will guide you to him and join you as soon as I have freed a young man who is being held captive as you were. There is nothing to fear . . . if you trust me completely. Will you . . . can you . . . do that?"

He was bending down so low that his eyes were on a level with mine and seemed to widen a little as I met his gaze.

"Yes, Bobby," I said. "I can—and will."

13 JOHN DYSON

WE ALL BEGAN to run at once. It was foolish, of course, but Laura seemed determined to keep a tight grip on my hand, even though she must have known that two people, running side by side, can make faster progress if they force themselves to forget that they are not alone.

In one way it was bad. But in another way the feeling of closeness which it gave us was very important and precious to us, and to have snatched my hand away would have been unthinkable, even though it was her safety I was most concerned about.

If it hadn't been for Bobby, who had waited to make

141

sure there was no danger that any of us would be left behind we might never have reached the sunlight. He's told Laura he had only one other prisoner to free, but must have discovered that there were four in all, because two youngish-looking men and a woman I recognized instantly—she was a waitress in a Wilmot Street luncheonette—emerged from the cave with us.

Bobby was still in the cave, but into my mind he had sent a warning message. It was as if I could hear his boyish voice calling out to me and the others must have been warned as well, for they were running as swiftly as we were toward a dark stretch of woodland that ran parallel with the cave on the opposite side of an acre-wide clearing.

Bobby's warning had been so grimly urgent that I feared he might still be standing where we had left him, between a pulsing core of darkness that almost blotted out the sunlight in a cavern open to the sky, and the same world outside the cave.

Their sleep is different from ours. When they have exhausted their energies they become somnolent in a dreamless, totally inhuman way. They are trapped still in that self-imposed somnolence but now the awakening is coming fast. The slumberous coils are unwinding and they are becoming more alert.

Get out of the cave and keep on running. Put as much distance as you can between their minds and yours. I will erect a barrier that will keep them from reaching out confusedly to overtake and destroy you before their awakening is complete. When once it is complete, when they are fully awake, the danger will be greater and I will have to oppose them with the full strength of my mind. I will be in very great danger then, for the mental force that they can summon to their aid may be too powerful for me to over-

142

*come. But I do not think that it will be. Get as
far away as you can and if the ground begins to
vibrate throw yourselves down and do not look in
the direction of the cave. The light may be blinding.*

We hadn't quite reached the edge of the woods when
we felt the first tremor. It was so faint that it did not
seem alarming and when Laura did not stop or hesitate
I kept right on running, feeling that if by taking a slight
risk we could cover the fifty or sixty feet that still sepa-
rated us from the woods it would be foolish not to attempt it. The second tremor was more violent and we realized that we'd made a mistake in ignoring Bobby's warning.

We both stopped running and threw ourselves down,
still holding hands, but not even pausing to exchange
startled glances. For an instant I heard only Laura's
harsh breathing, the scrape of my shoes against the sandy
soil as I flattened myself. Then another tremor came, so
violent that my shoulders jerked and I had to let go of
Laura's hand. Before I could reach out and clasp it again
there was a sudden, crackling sound, followed by three
thunder-loud explosions.

The first blast was so deafening that if the second and
third had not been even more thunderous I'm quite sure
I would not have heard them at all.

My ears were still ringing when I twisted about and
raised myself on my elbows. Laura had struggled to a
sitting position and was shaking her head, as if she, too,
had been half-deafened by the blast. There was a stunned
look in her eyes and she was staring skyward as if completely unaware that I had come back to life at her side.

The sky was laced with flame and the glare was still
so blinding that I had to shut my eyes again and keep
them shut for a moment.

The instant I opened them I saw it. Shining, silvery
and immense, it was rising straight up into the sky di-

143

rectly above Gower Cavern. It was revolving slowly as it ascended and so great was its beauty, so miraculous its symmetry, that it brought a catch to my throat.

As if in answer to what I couldn't help thinking words formed in my mind. "Yes, Mr. Dyson. It *is* beautiful. They are cold and alien and strange and have little love for the human race. But there is a splendor in them as well. I do not think that they will ever return. They know now that I am not alone on Earth—that there is a new kind of man who will increase in numbers as the years pass and that Earth can not be conquered as easily as they allowed themselves to believe."

It was Laura who saw him first, a Bobby Jackson still outwardly unchanged. She tugged at my arm and pointed and I saw him too—and stopped staring up into the sky. He had left the cave and was running straight toward us across the clearing, his tousled hair whipped by the wind.

THE END

www.ingramcontent.com/pod-product-compliance
Lightning Source LLC
Chambersburg PA
CBHW031129210626
46816CB00015B/1252